"Okay, Conner  u know how his mon ? Well, he's going to ships for you! If e Stanford bound." She grinned at Angel, waiting for him to hug her or kiss her or at least react.

"Tell him not to bother," Angel said.

Not quite the reaction she was going for.

"Excuse me?" she asked, leveling him with an incredulous stare. "Anyone taken your temperature lately?"

Angel clapped. "Sit down, Tee," he said. "I have news."

Baffled, Tia just dropped onto the bed. Angel knelt beside her and grabbed her hands in his.

"All right. This is getting weird," she said, her heart pounding with an as-yet-unfounded concern. "Tell me what's going on."

Angel locked eyes with her and took a deep breath. "I've decided I'm not going, Tia," he blurted out. "Forget Stanford. I'm going to stay here with you."

Don't miss any of the books in SWEET VALLEY HIGH
SENIOR YEAR, an exciting new series from Bantam Books!

Visit the Official Sweet Valley Web Site on the Internet at:

http://www.sweetvalley.com

Francine Pascal's SVH senioryear

Broken Angel

CREATED BY
FRANCINE PASCAL

BANTAM BOOKS
NEW YORK · TORONTO · LONDON · SYDNEY · AUCKLAND

RL 6, age 12 and up

BROKEN ANGEL

A Bantam Book / November 1999

Sweet Valley High® is a registered trademark of Francine Pascal.
Conceived by Francine Pascal.
Cover photography by Michael Segal.

Produced by 17th Street Productions,
a division of Daniel Weiss Associates, Inc.
33 West 17th Street
New York, NY 10011.

ISBN: 0-553-49282-9

Published simultaneously in the United States and Canada

Bantam Books are published by Bantam Books, a division of Random
House, Inc. Its trademark, consisting of the words "Bantam Books" and
the portrayal of a rooster, is Registered in U.S. Patent and Trademark
Office and in other countries. Marca Registrada. Bantam Books, 1540
Broadway, New York, New York 10036.

PRINTED IN THE UNITED STATES OF AMERICA

OPM   0 9 8 7 6 5 4 3 2 1

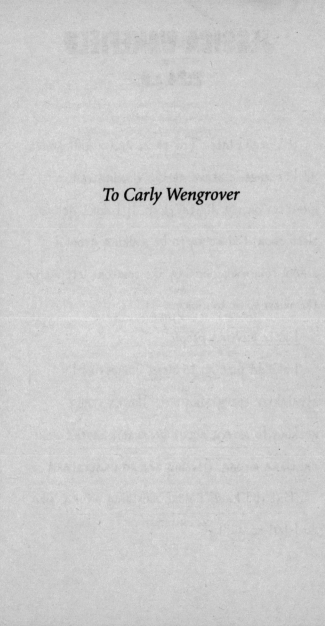

To Carly Wengrover

JESSICA WAKEFIELD
2:24 A.M.

It's really late. For three and a half hours all I've done is stare at the glowing red numbers on my digital clock. If I don't get to sleep soon, I'm going to be walking around school tomorrow looking like someone left me in the microwave too long.

I hate hurting people.

I should just go to sleep. Tomorrow I'll straighten everything out. There's really nothing to worry about because I haven't done anything wrong. Jeremy has to understand.

But if I haven't done anything wrong, why do I feel so guilty?

TIA RAMIREZ

2:27 A.M.

WHEN ANGEL DIDN'T SHOW UP TO
HANG OUT WITH ME AND CONNER, I WAS
SO MAD. I'D SPENT THE EARLY EVENING
ON EMERGENCY BABY-SITTING DUTY, AND
ALL I WANTED WAS TO KICK BACK WITH
MY BEST FRIEND AND MY BOYFRIEND
AND RELAX. BUT ANGEL WAS A NO-
SHOW.

I FIGURED THEY'D CALLED HIM TO
WORK A SHIFT AT THE RIOT AND HE
FORGOT TO TELL ME. AFTER ALL, THAT'S
ALL HE'S BEEN DOING LATELY—WORK.
IT'S LIKE THE ONLY WAY WE CAN SPEND
TIME TOGETHER IS IF I BUY A DRINK
FROM HIM.

THEN CONNER BRINGS ME TO THE
TRACK TO LOOK FOR HIM. I THOUGHT HE
WAS OUT OF HIS MIND. NO WAY WOULD
ANGEL BE HANGING OUT THERE WITH ALL
THE LOWLIFES. NOT MY BOYFRIEND.

BUT THERE HE WAS. AND THAT WASN'T
THE WORST PART. I HAD NO IDEA WHAT I
WAS IN FOR.

CONNER MCDERMOTT
2:29 A.M.

Angel has that blank stare.
I've seen it before, on my mother.
Whenever I catch her with a drink in
her hand.

CHAPTER

A Splash of Cold Water

1

Angel Desmond shifted on the hard wooden bleacher, staring at a crack in the floor between his feet. His girlfriend, Tia Ramirez, hovered over him, the bright racetrack lights combining with her form to cast a shadow over his face. He couldn't even lift his chin to meet her shocked, disappointed gaze. The guilt was too heavy.

Conner McDermott, the other friend who had shown up just in time to witness Angel's worst life moment, stood directly in front of Angel.

"When you say you lost all your money . . . what exactly do you mean by that?" Conner asked.

Now Angel was staring at Conner's beat-up work boots. "I mean I've lost everything," he replied, briefly glancing up at Conner's clouded green eyes. "My entire savings account is cleaned out. I have nothing." His voice diminished into a hoarse whisper.

"Please tell me this is some kind of sick joke," Tia demanded. Angel flinched at the harsh tone in her voice. Her brown eyes were wide, and her beautiful, olive skin had turned pale. "Answer me, Angel! Tell me what the hell happened!"

Angel fought the urge to run and hide, to streak off into the darkness as fast as his legs could propel him—faster, certainly, than any of the horses he'd bet on that night. At that moment he had no idea which was more painful: realizing the severity of his situation or seeing the devastated expression on Tia's face.

For as long as they'd been a couple, Angel had never seen her look at him this way. Like he was some kind of criminal instead of her boyfriend. It tore right into his heart. He wanted to say something—anything—to soften that look.

"Tia," he began, "I . . . I . . ." *Good,* he thought. *Very articulate.*

Tia shook her head slowly. "You what?" she asked. "Say something!"

Angel stared down at the grimy floor, made colorful by a mosaic of scattered betting receipts. Hundreds of scraps of paper representing hundreds of wasted hopes—not to mention thousands of wasted dollars.

"I . . . I was on a streak!" he blurted out, realizing how lame his reply sounded. "Everything was just fine! But then my luck just . . . turned or something."

Tia let out an exasperated sigh and brought one hand to her forehead. "I don't get it," she said, glancing at Conner as if he held the answers. Conner just shook his head and looked away. "This isn't like you, Angel," Tia continued. "You would never, *ever* do something like this. I mean, what were you thinking? What?"

He opened his mouth to reply, then immediately closed it again. What could he say anyway? He hadn't been thinking—at least not effectively. There had only been an overwhelming hope that his bets would pay off, just like they had before. But there was no way he could explain all that.

Tia climbed down over the bleacher in front of Angel and stood next to Conner. "Talk to me! Make me understand!"

Angel just stared back at her, letting her angry words wash over him as Conner wandered off a bit. Angel wished she would just go away. Who told them to show up anyway? Here he was in the middle of a living nightmare, and they had to walk in uninvited.

"You weren't here!" he said through clenched teeth. "I had it all under control!"

Tia's mouth fell open. "What does *that* mean? Obviously you *didn't* have it under control or you wouldn't be broke!"

"Hey, Tee," Conner said, walking over to her and placing his hand on her upper arm. Angel felt a slight sense of relief.

"What?" Tia snapped.

"Look, he already knows he screwed up royally," Conner replied calmly.

Gee, thanks, Angel thought. *Way to stick up for me.*

"But this doesn't make any sense!" Tia shouted, yanking her arm away from Conner. "There must be some mistake! You didn't actually lose *all* of your money, right? I mean, there's gotta be some left."

Angel felt as if she had shoved her hand through his chest and twisted his heart. He looked past her at the quiet racetrack. "I don't believe this!" she spat.

For a moment no one spoke. Angel could only hear the pounding of his heart and the whistling of a nearby janitor. Eventually Tia grabbed his shoulder and turned him around to face her.

"What are you going to do now?" she asked shakily.

The question reverberated through Angel's head. What *could* he do? Obviously turning back time was not an option. Other than that, he was fresh out of ideas.

Angel sighed heavily. "I'm going to the rest room," he mumbled. Then he stood shakily and climbed the bleachers before Tia could say anything further.

"Hey, pal. We're closed," one of the employees called out gruffly.

"Don't worry," Angel answered. "Just give me two seconds and I'll be out of here." *Forever,* he added silently.

4

He pushed through the squeaky door of the bathroom and took a deep breath of the foul-smelling air. Every step echoed off the tile walls as he made his way over to the line of sinks. He imagined himself a prisoner, taking his final walk to the gas chamber and certain death. *Not too far off the mark,* he thought. *In a few hours I'll have to face Dad.*

Angel turned on the cold faucet and splashed his face with handfuls of icy water. He wanted to wake himself up—to somehow dissolve the nightmare around him. But it didn't work. He was still there. Still broke. Still left without a future. The nightmare was real.

He turned off the tap and stood up straight, staring at his face in the mirror. His bloodshot eyes stared back, and droplets of water ran down his cheeks like heavy perspiration. He watched as they zigzagged around the thick stubble on his chin before falling into the sink below.

No wonder Tia's looking at me that way, he thought. *I look like a crazed asylum escapee.*

If only. That would make everything easier to explain. He could tell his parents he'd temporarily lost his sanity and ended up squandering his future at the track. At least then he'd have something to blame it on. Something besides his own stupidity.

Angel's throat tightened as he thought about all the times he'd overheard his father bragging to his customers about how "his boy" was going to

Stanford. And just a few days earlier his mother had surprised him with a Stanford University sweatshirt—a really expensive one. Now that money was squandered too.

"You let them down, man," he said to his reflection. "Mom and Dad believed in you, and you let them down."

How in the world was he going to tell them? If Tia could freak this much, how would his folks react? Would they scream and yell? Throw knives? Banish him from the house?

It doesn't matter, he thought, dabbing his face with a paper towel. *Whatever they do to me, I deserve it.*

"Tia. Take a breath. It's all right."

"It's not just the betting, Conner," Tia said brokenly. "It's . . . how could he have kept this from me?"

Tia paced the stands nervously. She was restless, but her activity was mainly powered by the hundreds of thoughts that raced through her head, each vying for attention simultaneously.

"Will you please stand still?" Conner said. "I can't talk to you if I can't even get a visual hold on you."

Tia ignored him. She felt schizophrenic. She wanted to undo the jumble of emotions inside her and sort them into neat little piles. First there was the overwhelming shock at what Angel had done.

Then there was the terror of what would happen now. And finally a paralyzing sympathy for Angel and how he must feel.

"How could he let this happen?" she whispered.

"Who knows?" Conner replied.

Tia winced at the sound of his voice. She'd almost forgotten he was standing there.

"I never saw this coming," he continued. "I mean, I knew he'd come back here a couple of times, but I didn't really think he'd—"

"You knew?" Tia shouted.

"Uh . . . yeah," he replied.

Tia shoved him. He didn't even flinch. "Why didn't you tell me?"

"Because I didn't think it was a big deal," he protested, stuffing his hands into the pockets of his brown suede jacket. "I never thought he'd do something like this."

Something like this. Tia shuddered at the phrase. Even Conner, who was nothing if not direct, couldn't say the words. *Lose all his money.* Tia's head slumped forward into her hands, her long, dark hair forming a curtain across her face.

"God, what a mess," she mumbled. "This is real, isn't it? He really lost everything."

"Don't panic." She could tell Conner was trying to make his gruff voice soothing. "At least he still has his scholarship."

"Yeah, but that won't pay for everything. It'll

cover tuition, but what about food? What about books? What about living expenses?" She shook her head and resumed her agitated wandering in front of Conner. Her heart felt as if it were going to explode from her chest. "What am I supposed to do?"

"Wait a minute," Conner said, holding out his hands. "This is Angel's deal. *He's* the one who has to do something. You just have to . . . do the supportive-girlfriend thing."

She stopped and glared at him. "I can't just do nothing."

"Tee, you can't fix this for him," Conner said.

She shut her eyes in an attempt to block out the truth of what he was saying. "Maybe I could talk to someone here. I could just explain that it was a mistake. He didn't mean to bet it all. He just got carried away."

She had turned and started walking toward the ticket office when Conner's voice stopped her.

"Are you going to be joining the land of the rational anytime soon?" he asked. "*No one* means to bet it all."

"Then what?" Tia asked. "What can I do?"

Conner sighed and raked his hand through his dark, messy hair. "Chill out and back off."

Tia rolled her eyes and crossed her arms over her chest, struggling to hold in a wave of tears.

Conner tucked in his chin and blew out an audible sigh. "Look, all I'm saying is . . ." He looked off toward the bathroom. "I don't think Angel's ready to face this. Not yet. It has to sink in."

"Fine," Tia said sharply, blinking back the tears. "If he's not ready, then *we* have to sit down and straighten this out for him. You and me. Because I am *not* gonna let this go."

Ken stood on the opposing team's thirty-yard line. He could smell the wetness on the grass, the muggy cloud of perspiration surrounding the players, and the faint tang of snack-bar corn dogs.

A roar welled up from the crowd in the stands. "Matthews, Matthews!" they chanted. Slowly the voices merged into one all-encompassing sound.

He knew they were waiting for the big play. It was time to concentrate.

He crouched behind the center and called for the snap. Then suddenly everything started happening in slow motion. The ball drowsily sprang up into his grasp. Players pushed and pivoted and raised their limbs in their low-speed running, making them look more like ballerinas than high-school jocks.

Ken took several strides back, peered over his linemen, and spotted a man wide open in the end zone. Keeping his eye on the receiver, he pulled back his arm and launched the pass. . . .

Then the world flipped inside out and Ken was the one standing in the end zone. Two opponents were rushing at him from opposite directions. Looking up, he saw the football spiraling down toward him like a guided missile. He raised his hands and snatched it out of the air.

The crowd thundered their elation. An announcer blared something incomprehensible over the PA. His teammates raced over and lifted him onto their shoulders.

He was so high up, he could see his whole family cheering him on in the packed stands. Maria was there too, her smile lighting up the stadium like a beacon. And there was someone sitting next to her.

Olivia. Clapping and whistling for him the way she always used to. Then she looked at Maria, smiled, and disappeared. . . .

"No!" Ken Matthews bolted upright in his bed. His heart was racing, and his forehead was covered with sweat.

He hadn't seen Olivia in so long. Her smile, her eyes, the way she tilted her head just slightly when she smiled. He'd pored over plenty of photographs since she died. But they were all frozen, lifeless. He felt he'd really seen her just now, the way she had been.

It hurt. Was it the reminder of her that hurt? Or was it guilt that he was starting to forget certain details? And why had Maria been there? Just the thought of Maria's presence made him feel guilty. Since Olivia, no other girls had made appearances in his dreams.

And then there was the whole football thing. He had to let that go. Coach Riley had made it clear there was no way he was getting back on the team. He didn't need to torture himself with fantasies of a game-saving play.

Ken rubbed his eyes, trying to erase any residual images from his mind. He should just go back to sleep and start over. Forget this ever happened.

He pounded his pillow and slowly settled back down on the mattress. But a creeping apprehension prevented him from completely relaxing, as if he'd lost something or failed to do some important task.

"Just chill," he told himself. "It was only a dream."

Will Simmons

You want to know one of the things I like best about football? I like that the game is clear and simple. We're the good guys, and the other team is, basically, the bad guys. We want to win. They have to lose. And whoever scores the most points is the winner. Easy, right?

Unfortunately real life isn't so simple.

I've wanted Jessica since school started, and now that she and Jeremy have broken up, there's nothing in my way. Good, right? Wrong. Because I'm the reason they busted up.

On the one hand, I'm glad she's available. But I also can't shake the sight of her crying after Aames stormed out. She must like the guy more than I thought. That sucks.

There just aren't any clear-cut rules here. I want to take advantage of this opportunity, but there's no guarantee things will turn in my favor. Plus Jessica has been almost happy around school lately, and I don't want to take that from her — again.

But I can't let things hang like this. I've got to do something. If we could get together, I _know_ I could make her happy. But what should I do now? What's my next play? After everything that's happened, I'm not sure where I stand.

Am I ahead in the game? Or did I just fumble?

It's too close to call.

CHAPTER
Face Your Fears

2

"Okay. You can do this, Jess. It's just Jeremy. He has to let you explain."

Jessica glanced at her image in the Jeep's rearview mirror one last time, then hopped out and quickly strode into House of Java. Her heart hammered in her ears at five times the speed of her footsteps. So much for remaining cool.

A tinkling of the New Agey chimes hanging on the door announced her presence. Jeremy glanced up from the espresso machine and did a double take. He looked incredible. His dark hair was tousled, and he was in need of a shave, but he was still incredible.

Jessica had hoped to see his face involuntarily light up, the way it usually did when he saw her. But it didn't. Instead he quickly averted his eyes and turned his back to her. Jessica felt like she'd been stabbed.

What do I do now? she wondered, pausing in midstride. *Should I just leave?*

"Jessica!" Ally Scott's brown ponytail popped up

15

from behind the counter. "You're not on the schedule today."

"I—uh—I only stopped by for a cappuccino," Jessica stammered.

"Just a social call, huh?" Ally said with a grin.

"Right. I mean . . ." Jessica paused and stared at Jeremy's back. "I just thought I'd come in and say hi."

Jeremy turned around and gave her a weary look. Obviously he was still too upset to talk. She should just cut her losses and leave—try again some other time.

"Hey, Al," Jeremy said, causing Jessica to freeze in place. "Would it be all right if I sit and talk with Jess for a sec?"

Ally glanced up at the clock and nodded. "Sure. We still have a few minutes before we open."

Jessica's heart jumped excitedly. Maybe he'd thought about everything and realized he had to hear her out. Jeremy quickly poured himself a cup of coffee and fixed Jessica a cappuccino. She smiled as she watched him add a few shakes of chocolate sprinkles on top—just the way she liked it.

"Let's go into the courtyard," he said quietly as she followed him around the tables. "I think Ally has her sonar on today."

They sat down at a corner table and faced each other. Up close, Jeremy's haggard expression showed Jessica he hadn't completely shrugged things off.

And after a long moment of awkward smiles and napkin twisting, she realized he was waiting for her to speak first.

Just do it! she told herself. *The sooner you tell him, the sooner things can go back to normal.*

She took a deep breath and stared into his eyes. "It wasn't a date."

Jeremy scratched at the back of his neck. "Jessica—"

"I *know* how it looked, but you didn't give me a chance to explain," she said, gaining speed and volume with every word. "We were just planning this big breakfast thing the cheerleaders and football players do every year. And it wasn't supposed to be just us either. Tia was going to be there, but then she got stuck baby-sitting. I know it looked like I was out *with* him, but really we were just working as a group—only the group sort of shrank down to the two of us at the last second."

"You do realize how made up that sounds," Jeremy said. He twisted his cup around on the saucer, staring at it intently.

"Yeah, I do," Jessica said with a sigh. "But I swear it's the truth. And I wish you would trust me. But if you don't, you can always ask Tia. You can even ask Liz. She took the message when Tia canceled, and *everyone* trusts her."

Jeremy leaned back in his chair and looked at her. "I don't have to call anyone," he said. "I thought about it last night, and I can't explain why, but I actually do believe you."

"You do?" Jessica asked, her blue-green eyes widening.

"Gut feeling," Jeremy said.

For a moment Jessica felt as if she were filling with helium, but then she realized that Jeremy wasn't smiling. In fact, he was staring at the scratched tabletop as if it held the meaning of life.

"What?" Jessica asked, her insides feeling hollow.

"It's just . . ." He glanced up at her for a split second and looked away. He couldn't hold her eye. *This is not good,* Jessica thought, crossing her arms over her chest protectively. *This is so not good.*

He was staring at the same spot. "It's just, I don't think I can be with you anymore . . . at least . . . right now," he said.

A chill shot through Jessica, and her grip on herself tightened. "But . . . why?"

"Because I think you like Will."

Jessica went numb. She tried to swallow, but she couldn't. "You what?"

He finally looked at her. His brown eyes were pained, hopeful, and desperate all at once. "And I can't be with you if you really want to be with someone else," he said flatly.

Jessica shook her head. "But I *don't* want to be with him! How could you even think that? After everything he put me through?"

"Hey, I don't get it either," he snapped. "But no matter what you say, you two looked really . . . couplelike last night. And you always act nervous when we see him. Obviously there's *something* there."

Jessica stared at Jeremy, dumbfounded. This wasn't supposed to happen. She'd come in to apologize, even though she hadn't technically done anything wrong. And now he was going to punish her even further? It didn't make sense.

Even if she was, in a bizarre, masochistic way, attracted to Will, so what? She wanted Jeremy. She'd *chosen* Jeremy. Somehow she had to make him understand that.

"You're wrong," she said, her voice and eyes pleading. "I mean, I am nervous when I'm around Will. But only because of the stuff he pulled on me. That's all."

"Really?" he asked, frowning. "Then why did you save all his gifts?"

Jessica was stung. "I . . . I just hadn't gotten around to throwing that junk away. You're making a big deal out of nothing, Jeremy. This whole thing—"

"Stop," he said tersely, making Jessica wince. Then he closed his eyes, took a deep breath, and softened his features. "Look, I just think we should take a break. You need to figure all this stuff out."

An aching helplessness crushed through her. "But . . . for how long?" she mumbled.

Jeremy shrugged wearily. "As long as it takes."

Angel lay in bed, staring at the patterns in the stucco ceiling. He had no idea how long he'd been lying there thinking, but he guessed it had been a few hours. He wasn't sure if he'd slept at all.

Maybe he had. Maybe the awful events at the track had only been a nightmare—some weird dream brought on by spicy food.

No such luck. One look in his empty wallet lying on his bedside table showed him it was real.

He forced himself upright and slid out from under the covers. Sunlight streamed in through his bedroom window, but it was harsh. Even his favorite Michael Jordan poster seemed to be leering at him disdainfully.

Angel pulled on his clothes and made his way downstairs. Then he paused in the doorway to the kitchen, sucked in his breath, and stepped through the threshold. Time to face the really depressing music.

"Well, good morning, sleepyhead! 'Bout time you got up. Come join us." Angel's mother smiled from behind her coffee mug. Her short, dark curls bobbed around her dimpled cheeks as she patted the seat next to her.

Why does she have to look so happy? Angel thought.

20

His father lowered the morning newspaper and frowned at him through his wire-rimmed glasses. "Finally. I was beginning to wonder whether you even came home last night. Thought maybe you and Tia decided to elope and give me a heart attack."

Angel stumbled over to the table and gave a fragile smile. *It wouldn't be the worst thing you could hear from me,* he thought.

His dad squinted at him. "What's the matter, son? Your tongue still asleep? Can't you say good morning?"

"Sorry," he mumbled. "Good morning."

"Although it's barely morning," his father continued, burying his face in the paper again. "You know, when I was a boy, I never had the luxury of sleeping late. I always had work to do. Always. No time to laze around."

"Don't listen to Mr. Gloom and Doom." Angel's mother stood up and kissed him on the cheek. "What's wrong, honey? Don't you feel well?"

"I'm just tired, I guess. I . . . didn't sleep well last night."

She smiled and patted him on the shoulder. "You need to eat something. I already cleared away breakfast, but I can get you some cereal if you like."

"Sure. Thanks," Angel said. But he wasn't in the mood for food. In fact, he wasn't in the mood to engage in any sort of normal function—not when everything inside him felt so abnormal.

21

His mother began flitting around, handing him a bowl, a spoon, a box of Wheaties, and the milk carton, humming to herself all the while. Angel could barely look at her. She seemed so happy and serene. Little did she know her own son had just ruined his life.

"So how did your date with Tia go last night?" his mother asked in her cheerful, singsongy voice.

"Um . . . not well," Angel answered distractedly. An image of Tia's stricken face loomed before him, almost collapsing his stomach.

Mrs. Desmond sighed and sat back down in her chair. "Well, I know it must be really hard for her right now. Just a couple more months and you'll be leaving for Stanford."

"Uh . . . yeah," Angel mumbled.

"You shouldn't let that bother you, son." His father grunted as he turned a page in his paper. "Right now, you don't need a lot of distractions. You've got to focus on the future."

Angel tried to drown out his father's words by noisily dumping Wheaties into his bowl.

"Oh, Bill. Let him have some fun," he heard his mother say. "He's working so hard to save up money, he deserves a little break now and then."

Angel shoveled a huge spoonful of cereal into his mouth and chomped down on it. He could barely taste the stuff, but at least the crunching in his ears managed to muffle the conversation.

"That reminds me." His mother placed a hand on his forearm. "You know, honey, we still need to go buy stuff for your dorm room. If you have some extra cash, I saw a store that has a sale on small refrigerators. I thought you could get one to store drinks in and—"

"No!" Suddenly Angel couldn't stand it any longer. "I can't! I can't buy anything!"

His parents froze, staring at him as if he'd morphed into a stranger in front of their eyes.

"Lower your voice," his dad cautioned. "Just because you were up till all hours of the night doesn't give you the right to yell at your mother."

"It's all right," his mother cut in, some of the enthusiasm gone from her voice. "We don't have to do it today, Angel. If you have plans, we could go shopping tomorrow or—"

"You don't understand," Angel said hoarsely. "I can't go shopping today or any day, Mom. I don't have any money."

They blinked back at him, confused. "What do you mean by that?" his dad asked.

Angel took in a long breath.

"I mean I'm broke," he blurted out. "I . . . I lost my money."

"You did what?" his father bellowed, his eyes wide.

His mother's face drained.

Angel hung his head. "It's all gone."

"How?" his dad demanded. "How did this happen?"

The words were there. They were right in his mouth, but Angel couldn't say them.

"Answer me!" his father bellowed.

Angel closed his eyes. "At the track," he said quietly. "I lost it at the track."

For a brief moment no one said anything, and Angel could feel the tension penetrating his pores.

"No," his mother said, puncturing the silence. "This is not possible."

"I know I messed up, Mom. I'm sorry," he said softly. "But I can fix it. I'll double my hours at the shop to make it up. I'll work all the time."

"You will not!" his dad shouted.

Angel jumped. "What?"

"I am not having my customers pay good, hard-earned money just so you can throw it away at the track!" He pushed back his chair and stood up. "As far as I'm concerned, you can find some other job. You will not be working for me anymore."

Angel felt like he'd been body-slammed. "Dad, no," he whispered. "How could you do that to me?"

"I didn't do it to you," his father snapped. "You did it to yourself. The sooner you realize that, the better." He turned and stomped out of the kitchen. Angel's mother followed, breaking into faint sobs as she rushed down the hall to her room.

A heavy silence surrounded Angel like the eerie stillness that preceded a violent storm.

He had never felt so alone.

TIA RAMIREZ

WHEN I WAS REAL YOUNG, I KEPT BUGGING MY MOM FOR A LITTLE BROTHER OR SISTER. I HAD MY OLDER BROTHER, RICKY, AND HE ALWAYS GOT TO PICK ON ME. I THOUGHT IT WOULD ONLY BE FAIR FOR ME TO HAVE SOMEONE TO PICK ON.

THEN JESSE CAME ALONG, AND ALL WE DID WAS FIGHT. I MEAN, REALLY <u>FIGHT</u>. LATER MIGUEL AND TOMÁS WERE ADDED TO THE MIX, AND OUR HOUSE BECAME THE JUNIOR VERSION OF THE WWF. NOW RICKY HAS ESCAPED TO COLLEGE AND I HAVE THREE LITTLE BROTHERS WHO ARE ALWAYS GETTING INTO MY THINGS, INVADING MY PRIVACY, AND CALLING ME THOUGHTFUL NICKNAMES LIKE "BARF BREATH" OR "DINOSAUR BUTT." PLUS HAVING TO BABY-SIT THEM ALL THE TIME REALLY CUTS INTO MY SOCIAL LIFE. I MEAN, I LOVE THEM, BUT EVEN I CAN ONLY TAKE SO MUCH.

ANYTIME I COMPLAIN ABOUT IT,

THOUGH, MY MOM JUST SMILES AND SAYS, "BE CAREFUL WHAT YOU WISH FOR!" SMART WOMAN.

FOR MONTHS NOW I'VE BEEN SECRETLY HOPING SOMETHING WOULD HAPPEN SO THAT ANGEL WOULDN'T GO TO COLLEGE. OF COURSE, MY DAYDREAMS WERE ALWAYS REALLY POSITIVE. LIKE HE'D WIN THE LOTTERY AND BE SET FOR LIFE. OR STANFORD WOULD INEXPLICABLY DECIDE TO RELOCATE TO EL CARRO.

I NEVER, EVER WANTED SOMETHING BAD TO HAPPEN TO ANGEL. I MEAN, COULD I, IN SOME WAY, HAVE BROUGHT THIS ON HIM?

"BE CAREFUL WHAT YOU WISH FOR!"

I SWEAR, I SHOULD HAVE THAT TATTOOED TO MY EYELIDS.

Maria Slater

From: mslater@swiftnet.com
To: KenQB@swiftnet.com
Time: 4:31 P.M.
Subject: Hey!

Hey, Ken!

How did it go at practice? Did the coach let you back on the team? Remember that even if you have practice every day, you will not be ditching our study dates. If you do, I'll personally stand on the sidelines and nag you the entire game.

Hmmm. That might actually be sadistically fun.

Maria

Ken Matthews

From: KenQB@swiftnet.com
To: mslater@swiftnet.com
Time: 5:22 P.M.
Subject: Re: Hey!

Maria—

Practice did <u>not</u> go well. Coach told me it's too late. I already made my decision to quit, and that's final. So . . . looks like I'll have tons of time to study with you. Speaking of which . . . what do you say we meet tomorrow at the library? That quiz in English is coming up, and I could use some help . . . and I'll bribe you with ice cream.

Have you noticed I like to use . . . ?
WB

Ken

Maria Slater

From: mslater@swiftnet.com
To: KenQB@swiftnet.com
Time: 5:30 P.M.
Subject: Re: Re: Hey!

Ken—

Yes, I've noticed your love of ellipses. But at least you're not making stupid faces out of punctuation marks.

You're on for studying and ice cream, thank you very much.

Sorry about Coach. That really sucks. How are you doing?

Ken Matthews

From: KenQB@swiftnet.com
To: mslater@swiftnet.com
Time: 5:32 P.M.
Subject: Re: Re: Re: Hey!

:-(

CHAPTER
Play It Again
3

Ken pulled his Isuzu Trooper into the parking lot of the Sweet Valley YMCA. He was determined to break a sweat that day. Weight training, boxing, basketball—anything as long as he wasn't sitting around at home, watching videos of last year's home games.

He couldn't remember the last time he'd felt that rush of adrenaline and clarity of focus he always attained during a good workout. When Olivia died the past summer, he'd stopped working out. He couldn't bear to feel his heart pumping, knowing that Olivia's had stopped beating altogether.

His friends hadn't understood. Everyone kept suggesting he go toss a football around to get his mind off things—as if sports were some sort of solace to losing the girl you loved. For a long time he couldn't even stand the smell of perspiration or the sound of a cheering crowd. It had made him feel guilty.

But now everything was different. He hadn't gotten over Olivia, and he knew he never would completely, but at least he'd stopped beating himself up about surviving.

Ken stepped through the doorway and immediately spotted Todd Wilkins sitting at the front counter, wearing the standard YMCA-staff polo shirt.

"Hey, Wilkins!" Ken called out. "Since when do you work here?"

"Hey, man!" Todd greeted him with a nod. "I just started a couple of days ago. Thought the volunteer work would look good on my college applications. What brings you here?"

"Gotta stay in shape somehow," Ken said flatly.

Todd raised his eyebrows. "Yeah. It really sucks that Coach won't let you back on the team."

Ken felt a stab of disappointment but managed a cool shrug. "Yeah, well . . . I probably wouldn't do you guys much good. I've gone kind of soft over the past few weeks."

"I don't know." Todd sighed and stared off in the direction of the large gymnasium, where a basketball game was in full swing. "I was thinking you coming back would help with unity a little."

"I didn't think you needed any help," Ken said, frowning. "You have a great record so far."

"Yeah, but team spirit is actually getting worse," Todd said. "Lately those El Carro morons think they own the team. Everything has to be their way. We've even had some fights on the field."

"Man, that sucks," Ken mumbled. "But what about Will? He should be holding it all together."

Todd snorted disdainfully. "He's part of the problem. Like he's always calling plays for the El Carro receivers and he ignores us even if we're wide open. Coach freaked out on him the other day, and things have gotten a little better, but I don't know."

A knot of emotions unraveled inside Ken. He felt bad for his former teammates and guilty for having abandoned them, but he was also happy to hear that Wonder Boy Will wasn't having an easy time of it. He hadn't fully realized until recently how much it bothered him to see Will in his old position, and it was a small comfort that his replacement wasn't exactly improving on Ken's success.

"Coach should've given you a shot," Todd continued, shaking his head glumly. "You belong out there, man."

"Hey, mister!" A boy appeared next to Todd and held up a dented basketball. "This ball went flat."

"I'll be right there," Todd told him, then he turned back to Ken. "Well, I gotta start collecting equipment. I'll try to catch you later, okay?"

"Yeah. See ya," Ken called out as Todd disappeared into the gym.

You belong out there, Todd's words repeated in Ken's mind. Too bad Coach didn't agree with him.

Ken took a deep breath, walked down the hall, and pushed through the metal door leading to the exercise room. Inside, the familiar smell of sweat and humidity transported him back to the school locker room. He remembered the screaming pep talks, the celebrating, the way the heat of the showers numbed the aches and pains in his body. And he remembered the pride of doing something well. He missed that most of all.

Ken straddled a weight bench and began doing arm curls, starting off with a relatively light weight to get his muscles used to burning again. The steady rhythm of pumping iron had always been an effective way for him to unwind and think clearly.

Todd was right. He did belong on the team. It was *his* team—or at least half of it was. He'd taken them to the state championships last year. Now Coach probably wouldn't even let him sign on as water boy.

Lately his life had felt as deflated as that kid's basketball, and he couldn't take it anymore. Somehow he had to fill the void.

There had to be something he could do to be a part of the team again. He owed it to himself to at least give it another shot. Even if it meant more Riley-induced public humiliation.

"And so I just sat there," Jessica blabbed on, stretching out on the Fowlers' sofa. Since leaving Jeremy at House of Java, her stunned sorrow had turned into loud indignation, and she couldn't make herself shut up about the unfairness of it all. "Like, how am I supposed to prove to him that I care about him more than Will? I mean, it's not like I can set up some scenario where they're both drowning and I'm holding the only life jacket. Right?"

Jessica stared at the back of her sister's head. Elizabeth was sitting cross-legged on the floor, staring up at the flickering television. She didn't even move.

"Right," Jessica answered herself. "So I try to talk him out of this, but he won't listen. And the thing is, I haven't done anything wrong. Nothing! This whole Will thing is just a product of his out-of-control imagination. But does he listen? No-o. It's like pleading with a slab of granite. I mean, should I try power tools next or what?" She leaned over and waved her hand in front of her sister's face. "Liz? *Liz?*"

"What?" Elizabeth said with a frustrated sigh, her eyes fixed straight ahead.

"Are you even listening to me?"

"Jess, I thought we were watching a movie here."

Stung, Jessica felt her cheeks redden, and she sat back against the cushion with an insulted pout. "Excuse me if my problems are interfering with your important video viewing. How many times have you seen this anyway? About four thousand?"

Elizabeth's shoulders lifted and fell. "So what? It's a classic."

"Yeah. I know, I know," Jessica muttered. "It's

Casablanca! The greatest love story ever! Blah, blah, blah."

"God, Jess! You sound like Lila," Elizabeth said.

Jessica narrowed her eyes. Did she really sound *that* bad? All she wanted was a little attention after Jeremy kicked her in the gut and ripped out her heart. Was that so much to ask?

"Sorry," Jessica mumbled. "I guess I'm just not in a love-story sort of mood right now."

Elizabeth exhaled audibly and made a big, exaggerated show of picking up the remote and pausing the tape. Finally she turned around. "I *asked* you if this movie was okay, and you said it didn't matter."

Jessica gaped at her. "What is with you today? I'm having some real problems right now, and all you care about is your dumb movie."

She watched as Elizabeth's expression slowly clouded over. "Forgive me, Jess, if I'm not shedding tears about you feeling torn between *two guys*. There are worse things, you know."

Jessica detected the true feelings beneath her sister's mocking tone. How could she be babbling on about Jeremy and Will when Elizabeth was still torn up about the whole Conner thing?

"You're lucky, you know," Elizabeth added, her voice sad and distant. She was staring at the coffee table. "Jeremy could have totally written you off."

"Look. Let's just forget about it," Jessica said quickly. "The important thing is that we're having a

36

girls' night. Just you and me. We haven't done that in a while."

"Yeah, well, this is the first time in over a week that you didn't cancel on me," Elizabeth muttered, turning toward the TV again.

Jessica's blood boiled at Elizabeth's uncharacteristically acidic tone, but she told herself to let it go. Her sister did have a point.

"Hey, that ends here," Jessica said. "So what if we don't have dates on a Saturday night? I mean, it's not the end of the world. It's not like we don't have lives, right?"

"Right," Elizabeth replied unemphatically.

Jessica grabbed a handful of popcorn from the bowl on the table. "We've got everything we need. Snacks, a VCR, Humphrey Bogart and Lauren Bacall—"

"It's Ingrid Bergman, not Lauren Bacall."

Jessica rolled her eyes. "Work with me here."

"Whatever," Elizabeth whispered wearily. She started the film.

Jessica slid off the couch onto the floor next to Elizabeth and handed her sister the popcorn bowl.

On the screen a beautiful woman was staring deep into Humphrey Bogart's eyes, a single tear sparkling on her cheek.

"So what's going on? What's her problem?" Jessica asked, mesmerized by the woman's look of desperation.

"She's in love with him," Elizabeth answered impatiently.

"Does he love her?"

"Yes!"

Jessica frowned. "So what's the problem?"

Elizabeth rolled her eyes. "She's married to Paul Henreid, who's a big leader in the underground-war-resistance movement. He's a great guy—an important guy. And Bogart's trying to tell her she should stay with him, no matter what their feelings for each other, because it would be better for everyone in the long run."

"So . . . she's torn between the man she loves and the man who's best for her?" Jessica asked, the little hairs on her arms standing on end.

"Uh-huh," Elizabeth grunted.

Jessica flopped down on her stomach and rested her chin in her hands. Maybe she should watch this movie after all. Somehow it all sounded very familiar.

Tia stood with her back to the bar at the Riot. Behind her, Angel mechanically wiped down dripping glasses fresh from the washer. She casually sipped her Coke and talked to him, keeping her eye out for Mr. Walker, the manager, who was tending bar upstairs. As dorky as she felt, she knew this was the only way of conversing with Angel without risking his much-needed job.

"So, what did they say, Angel?" she asked casually. "I mean, how exactly did your mom and dad react?"

"It was a disaster," Angel replied drearily. "Mom totally freaked, and Dad fired me from the shop."

"What?" She started to turn around but caught herself in time. "Is he mental?" she hissed. "You need that job more than ever now!"

"Tell me about it," he muttered.

"You've got to talk to him, Angel," she said.

"Yeah, right. I'd be better off talking to this concrete floor."

His tone was so defeated, Tia couldn't help but pivot around to face him. "You've got to at least try," she urged. "He's just really angry right now, but you can't give up."

"You know how my dad is," he snapped. "He's *not* going to listen."

"Angel—"

"Can we drop it?"

Tia leaned against the bar and rested her forehead in her hands, staring at the cup-ring-dotted counter. She felt paralyzed with frustration. How did Angel expect to get out of this if all he did was stand around and pout? Did he think things were going to work themselves out on their own?

"So . . . how was the game this afternoon?" he asked, sounding completely void of interest.

Tia sighed. "We won. Barely," she muttered, turning

back around. "Took advantage of their turnovers."

"Glad to hear someone's having a run of good luck."

The edge in his voice made Tia cringe. She reached out and laid her hand on his arm. "It's going to be all right, Angel," she said, trying to force as much faith into the statement as possible.

He shrugged one shoulder.

"I mean it," she pressed on. "We're going to figure this out."

Angel exhaled audibly through his nose and pulled away from her, leaving her hand feeling tingly, warm, and unbelievably empty.

"Listen, I have to get back to work before I get booted out of here too," he said. "I'll catch you later." He barely even looked at her before disappearing into the kitchen.

Trying to keep herself from bursting into frustrated tears, Tia turned and scanned the room for her friends. She tucked her hands under her arms. Conner and Andy should have been here by now. And man, did she need someone to vent to.

"You look less than happy."

Tia jumped and glanced over her shoulder. Conner was standing there wearing the McDermott smirk, and Andy Marsden was hovering just to his left, his curly red hair sticking out in even more directions than usual.

"So, who's in trouble?" Andy asked.

"You are," she replied coolly, starting off through the crowded table area and weaving her way toward the booths at the far wall. "Where have you guys been? I thought you were going to meet me here early," she called back.

"It is early," Conner said with a shrug as she paused next to an empty booth.

"So . . . any unusual mating rituals tonight?" Andy asked, rubbing his palms together. "What have we missed?"

Tia made a noise that fell somewhere between a sigh and a grunt. This was not the time for Andy's half witticisms or Conner's biting sarcasm. Right now she wanted sensitive, reassuring allies. Where were the girls when she needed them?

"Oh, nothing," she grumbled. "Angel's life is going down the toilet, and all I can do is watch him swirl around." She closed her eyes and tilted her head back and forth to crack her neck.

"Yeah. Uh . . . actually"—Andy brought his voice down to a repentant tone—"we were just talking about that."

"Let's sit," Conner said, sliding into the booth.

Tia plopped down across from them and gazed hopefully at their somber faces. "You guys don't have any ideas either, huh?" she asked.

"Not really," Andy replied defeatedly.

"I still don't think we have a part in this, Tee," Conner said. "This is Angel's deal."

"How can you say that?" Tia asked, leaning forward in her seat. "He's totally out of it, Conner. His folks freaked out on him today, and his dad fired him from the shop."

Andy whistled through his teeth. "Man, that sucks."

"It's really messing with him," Tia went on. "He's completely shut down."

"Sorry, Tee," Conner muttered, picking at the chipping paint at the edge of the black table. "This is just one of those things you can't fix."

"Will you stop being so cynical and think!" Tia cried. "We've got to come up with something."

"That's just it," Andy said, wrinkling up his freckled nose. "Conner and I talked about this for over an hour and couldn't come up with a single workable idea. It doesn't seem like there's much we can do except try to cheer the guy up."

Tia leaned back and let out a long, slow sigh. She knew they were right. How were any of them going to come up with the money Angel had lost in the short time he had to retrieve it?

She folded her arms on the table and dropped her head, feeling her long, brown ponytail flop over onto the table's rough surface.

"I wish we could just walk up behind some millionaire and club him over the head," Andy muttered. He picked up the tiny votive candle from the center of the table and tilted it, pouring hot wax onto the table.

Tia lifted her chin and rolled her eyes at him. "That was constructive."

"Wait a minute. . . ." Conner sat up straighter and looked at Andy thoughtfully.

"Uh . . . you aren't seriously thinking about mugging someone, are you?" Tia asked cautiously. "Because as happy as I am that you want to help, I think we should—"

"My mom," Conner said, narrowing his eyes as the wheels obviously started to turn.

"You want to mug your mother?" Andy asked, picking at the hardening wax with his thumbnail.

"No," Conner said. He looked Tia directly in the eye. "But we could probably use her."

Tia's heart took a little skip. "The charities," she said.

"Exactly." Conner smiled.

"You lost me," Andy said.

Tia pushed herself back in her seat as her mind started to race. "Conner's mom belongs to all of these clubs and charity organizations. You know those scholarships the school hands out at the end of every year?" Andy nodded. "Mrs. Sandborn's clubs fund half of those."

"Maybe Angel could apply and my mom could put in a good word for him," Conner finished.

"That's the first good plan I've heard all night," Andy said, grinning.

Tia could feel the pressure subsiding, as if a giant

43

fist had suddenly let go of her. "Conner, if you could do this—"

"I'll do what I can, Tee," Conner said. "But I'm not making any promises."

"It doesn't matter," she replied, beaming with gratitude. "At least it's a plan. And who knows? Maybe this is what Angel needs to bring him back to the land of the living."

Elizabeth Wakefield

Okay. I have now officially tried everything to cheer myself up. I've eaten entire boxes of chocolate-chip cookies. I've driven along the beach during sunset. I've even given money to those door-to-door faith bringers, thinking that an act of selflessness might bring me inner peace. Unfortunately, the only results I got from these methods were nausea, a stiff neck, and several pamphlets on finding enlightenment through whole-grain diets.

Even <u>Casablanca</u> didn't do the trick. I must be worse off than I thought.

It's like I've gone totally numb.

Nothing matters much anymore. Stuff that used to occupy my thoughts all the time has now been elbowed out of the way by memories of Conner. It's like I'm stuck in reverse. Right now I've got four days' worth of homework and two articles for the <u>oracle</u> to write. But every time I sit down at my desk, I space out, and the next thing I know, an hour has passed and all I've done is think about him.

Even Mom and Dad don't like me hanging around the house all the time. How pathetic is that? They keep nagging at me to find another part-time job. Mom keeps reading the help-wanted ads to me during breakfast, as if some notice about a baby-sitting position will make me dab my mouth with a napkin, jump up from the table, and fly out the door, resume in hand. She just doesn't understand. No one does. The only work I want right now is helping Conner. But that job is already filled—by Conner himself.

No one else need apply.

In the Name of 4riendship

Jessica lifted the metal scooper, turned toward the open coffee mill, glanced involuntarily at Jeremy, and proceeded to spill hundreds of Colombian Supremo beans all over her feet—for the second time that morning.

"Oh, no, no, *no!*" she moaned. "This isn't happening!"

Luckily, due to her earlier fumble, the broom was already leaning against the nearby wall. But as she reached out to grab it, Jeremy snatched it from her grasp.

"I'll do it," he said flatly.

Jessica could only stand and wallow in her embarrassment as he worked. At least he'd spoken to her. Since they began their shift at House of Java an hour ago, Jeremy had responded to all her attempts at conversation with polite nods and semismiles. Of course, the place had been busy. And Ally had been nosing around a lot. He was probably just feeling awkward—something she definitely understood at that moment.

47

"Thanks," Jessica said, grabbing the dustpan and kneeling behind the mound of beans. "I don't know what's wrong with me today. You think Ally somehow managed to turn up the gravity around here, thinking it would bring in customers?"

"Maybe," Jeremy mumbled, avoiding eye contact.

Okay. At least that was an answer.

"Or maybe these are, like, special kamikaze beans that would rather plummet to the floor than face the grinder," she added.

Jeremy glanced at her and quickly looked away. "*Colombian* jumping beans?" he said lightly. "I don't think so."

Jessica laughed, relieved. *Yes!* she cheered inwardly. *A real response!*

If only he would really look at her. It was hard to know the score when you couldn't see the other person's eyes.

Jessica took a deep breath and pressed on. "Anyway, thanks. Do you make a habit of helping out clumsy coworkers, or should I feel special?" She looked at him hopefully and pushed her blond hair behind her ear.

Jeremy only allowed half of his body to respond, lifting one shoulder and one corner of his mouth.

Oh, well, Jessica thought glumly. *Half a chance is better than nothing.*

She smiled tightly and dumped the beans in the garbage, wondering what to say next. Watching

48

Casablanca had helped convince her that she should never have let her attraction to Will—even subconsciously—distract her from Jeremy. He was the one she should be with. The one who actually cared about her and had proven it to her more than once. But how could she tell him that? What could she say to make him take her back?

Jeremy returned the broom to the nearby corner. As Jessica replaced the lid on top of the garbage can, she could see him look at her out of the corner of her eye.

It was the evidence she'd been searching for. The body language was unmistakable. He missed her.

Jeremy crossed over to the counter and leaned against the dark green surface, gazing out at the half-empty café. Jessica set down the dustpan and walked up to the counter beside him, pretending she was going back to her coffee grinding, but instead she turned to face his profile.

"Hey, Jeremy," she said softly. "Can we talk?"

"About what?" he asked, eyeing her warily.

"I just want you to know that I thought over everything you said yesterday. . . ." She reached out and shakily touched his forearm, unsure of how he would respond. He didn't move, but he was so tense, his skin actually felt taut. "I want to be with you, Jeremy. No one else."

There. She'd done it. Spilled it all out just like the coffee beans.

Jeremy exhaled slowly and pulled his arm away. "Don't do this, Jess," he mumbled.

"Do what?" she asked, awkwardly retracting her hand. "Didn't you hear what I said?"

"Yes."

"So . . ." She studied his clouded eyes, usually so clear and free of pretense. "What are you thinking?" she asked.

Jessica watched as his face grew tense, his forehead creasing up and his jaw locking. "I'm thinking one day isn't enough time. You need longer than that to really figure this out."

Jessica felt like she could jump out of her skin. "But there's nothing to figure out! That's what I'm trying to tell you. This is just a waste of time."

"It's not that easy, Jessica," Jeremy said in an odd tone that could only be called stern.

"It is for me," Jessica said, looking into his eyes. But they remained closed off. He wasn't giving her an inch.

He sighed heavily. "How can you be so sure when you won't even put it to the test? What are you so afraid of?"

Jessica's jaw dropped open as an indignant flush crept over her face. "How can you ask me that? You're the one who's scared. You're the one who's pushing me away for no reason."

"Well, if that's the case, then I'll know it soon enough, won't I?"

50

She stared at him in mute anger. Hot tears welled up in her eyes, blurring his face. How could he expect her to get through days or weeks or months of this when she wasn't sure she could endure the next two hours?

Jeremy took her hand gently and held her limp palm between his thumb and fingers. "If you're so sure I'm wrong, then prove me wrong," he said, his voice raspy.

It was more than Jessica could take. Tears began spilling down her cheeks, and her breath came in short gasps.

"So . . . what then?" she asked shakily. "Am I not allowed to see you? To even talk to you?"

"We'll be friends," he replied.

Jessica stared at him uncomprehendingly while a harsh pain sliced through her chest. She had the distinct feeling Jeremy was feeding her heart through the coffee grinder.

"Friends?" she repeated. "But—"

But she didn't get to finish. Right at that moment Ally burst out of the back office, and Jeremy dropped Jessica's hand. She could still feel the imprint of his thumb on her palm.

"Boy, things are dead right now," Ally said, scanning the café. She pulled the scrunchie out of her long, brown hair and started to redo her ponytail. "As long as we have this lull, could one of you go refill all the napkin dispensers?"

51

"I will," Jeremy quickly replied.

Jessica watched him turn and trudge into the dining area. Meanwhile her unspoken reply reverberated through her head.

But friends don't make you feel this awful.

Conner stared warily at the door to his mother's bedroom. He knew he should just stride right in and talk to her, but something kept his boots glued to the plush hallway carpeting.

It had been a long, long time since he'd asked a favor from anyone—especially his mother—and he didn't like the idea at all. Usually he could handle everything on his own. But this was one of those rare situations where he was completely powerless. And his mother, strangely enough, had some power.

Or she would if she could stay sober long enough to talk to her country-club pals.

Conner sighed. Why did those family sitcoms on television always make it look so easy? If he were one of those testosterone-challenged Brady boys, all he'd have to do was say, "Golly gee, Mom. My friend's in a real pickle. It would be really groovy if you could help him out." Then Mrs. Brady's shag hairstyle would be flapping in the breeze as she jumped in the station wagon to do her three-hundredth good deed of the day.

But the Bradys didn't quite have the same home life as the Sandborn-McDermotts. None of those TV families did. You never saw Richie Cunningham cleaning up his mother's vomit after an evening of club martinis. And none of the *Cosby Show* kids ever had to hand in an illegible signature on their report card because their mom had the shakes the morning she signed it.

Conner hated the predictably sweet, sappy endings on all those TV reruns. His life, at least, was never predictable. But it was rarely sweet either.

He should just do it. Just knock on the stupid door and get it over with. After all, his friend's future was in his hands.

No pressure there, he thought.

Conner closed his eyes, inhaled deeply, and rapped lightly on his mother's door. He expected a long silence or an incoherent moan in return. Instead a lilting, almost cheerful voice that sounded remarkably like his mother's replied.

"Come in!"

Good. So she was awake and seemingly in a pleasant mood. He opened the door and stuck his head inside.

"Conner, honey," his mother said, smiling sunnily. "How are you?"

"Uh . . . fine," he replied, taking in her neatly ironed outfit, carefully styled hair, and unsmudged lipstick. He hadn't seen his mother look so put together in weeks.

"Just a second, sweetheart," she said, turning back

toward the desk. "Let me finish this up, and I'll be right with you."

Honey? Sweetheart? Was she possessed?

Conner tried to steal a glance at what his mother was writing. Venturing closer, he could see she was making out a check to the utility company. A pile of other important-looking papers and envelopes lay next to her hand.

Conner blinked in amazement. He had to be seeing things. He hadn't thought his mother was aware that they still received monthly bills, it had been so long since she'd paid them. That was just one of the many responsibilities Conner had gradually taken on over the years.

But somehow she'd found this month's statements and was actually writing out checks. As he watched, he noticed her hand wasn't shaking at all, and her movements were too quick for someone who'd had a few morning nips from a booze bottle.

This was too perfect. Eerily perfect. Conner began to wonder if he'd somehow slipped into a very-Brady universe.

"There," Mrs. Sandborn said, placing a stamp on the utility-company envelope. "Now, what's up with you?" She turned and fixed him with another wide, happy smile.

Conner blinked and sat down on the bed behind him. It was too much. He was having serious trouble processing his immediate situation. Something wasn't right. Or actually, too many things were right.

"Conner?" his mother prompted.

"I . . . uh . . . I need to ask a favor," he began slowly, fairly certain he was going to wake up any second.

Mrs. Sandborn's expression grew simultaneously pleased and suspicious. "Really?"

"It's about Angel. He's supposed to be going to college soon."

Her eyes widened. "Is he? Already?"

Conner sighed. "He graduated from El Carro last spring. Remember?"

"Time flies," Mrs. Sandborn said.

When you're in a blackout half the time, Conner finished silently.

"Anyway, the thing is, he's not going to have enough money saved up for college after all, and time is running out," Conner explained.

His mother nodded patiently, a concerned frown creasing her features. She was actually focused. Weird.

Suddenly the words started shooting out of him like rapid gunfire. "Anyway, Angel's going to Stanford, and he has the grades, so I was thinking you could, maybe, talk to some of the right people in the right organizations to try and help him get a scholarship so he can still go."

Conner took a deep breath and wiped his palms

on his jeans. He knew his tone of voice was more appropriate for a heated debate than an urgent appeal, but he couldn't help it. He wasn't very skilled at asking for things.

His mother just sat there, staring at him. Suddenly all Conner wanted to do was get out of the room. He stood up abruptly and stuffed his hands in his front pockets.

"Just think about it," he said, backing away from the bed.

"Let me ask *you* something," Mrs. Sandborn said, freezing him in his tracks. "What made you decide to come ask me for help? Normally you're so big on doing everything by yourself."

"Normally I *have* to do everything by myself," Conner snapped. He couldn't help it. It was the kind of comment that was always on the tip of his tongue, just waiting for provocation.

Mrs. Sandborn's eyes narrowed. *Good job, man,* Conner chided himself. *You've just blown it.*

"I can do without the sarcasm," his mother said frostily. "But even so, I'll do what I can to help Angel." She reached into the top drawer of her desk and pulled out an address book. Flipping a few pages, she pointed to a number with her left index finger while picking up the phone with her right.

Conner stood watching in disbelief. His mom always seemed to have a thousand excuses why she couldn't or shouldn't do things.

"Don't look so surprised," his mother said, reading his expression as she pressed the phone receiver to her ear. "I just hope you remember I'm not so useless after all."

Let's see. . . . Multiply the number of weeks left before I leave for Stanford times the money I pull in at the Riot each week. . . . Take out taxes, gas money, and a very frugal twenty dollars a week for spending money. . . . And that leaves . . .

No way.

Angel hastily checked over his figures. According to the cold, hard numbers, it was going to take several more months to earn back his college money with his current wages. In other words, he was toast.

What if I increased my hours at the club? I could plead with Mr. Walker to enslave me full-time now that Dad canned me.

Angel quickly worked the numbers with his pencil. Forty hours a week? No. Still not enough. Sixty hours a week? Not even close. Just for curiosity's sake, he tried figuring out how much money he could save if he worked 24/7. That brought him closer to his target amount, something he could survive off of if he lived like a monk at Stanford.

Of course, there was no way he could pull it off. For one thing, the club was only open from 4 P.M. to 2 A.M. nightly, with a four-hour lunch shift on weekends. Plus even a penny-pinching slave driver like

Walker wouldn't work him that hard. There were probably strict laws against it.

But what if he found another job? Something that paid better than the Riot?

Again Angel hurriedly worked out the figures to find out what he'd need to make at forty hours a week in order to reach his target amount.

Divide by forty . . .

Carry the two . . .

Which came out to . . .

Eighteen dollars? Great. Now all he needed was to find someplace willing to hire a guy with no college degree, who would leave them in a matter of weeks, whom they felt deserved eighteen dollars an hour. Jeez. If he could get a job like that, who needed college anyway?

"Forget it," he mumbled. "It's over, man. Give in already."

Angel stared down at the sheet of numbers in front of him and sighed deeply. Obviously he'd mastered high-school math well enough to figure out that college was impossible. Why had he worked so hard for good grades anyway? They certainly didn't matter now.

With a growl of frustration he ripped the paper out of his notebook, wadded it up into a ball, and threw it across the room. It sailed in a perfect arc toward the wastepaper basket, hit the rim of the can, and bounced off onto the carpet.

Perfect, he thought glumly. *That about sums up my life.*

Angel crossed his arms on his desk and laid his head down, closing his eyes. There was only one hope left.

"Dear God," he whispered shakily. "Please tell me what I'm supposed to do. There's got to be some way I can make things right again. Just give me a sign."

For several minutes he sat there completely motionless and yet reaching with all his inner being for something to grasp onto. An idea or a plan—anything to prevent him from being swallowed up by the guilt.

And then finally he could breathe easier. And he could think.

As Angel slowly lifted his head and opened his eyes, his gaze landed on a familiar, beautiful face. A photo of Tia was smiling up at him from its golden oval frame.

Suddenly that was the only sign he needed.

He knew what he had to do.

Jessica Wakefield

Jeremy

Cons	Pros
—He wants to take a break.	—He's beyond cute.
	—He makes me laugh.
	—He's a good person who works hard to help his family.
	—He knows exactly how I like my coffee.
	—He's gentle, sweet, thoughtful, polite, and mature and looks amazing in his football pants.

Will

Cons	Pros

-Liar   -The way I feel when

-Ego with legs   I'm with him

-Liar

-He cheated on his

girlfriend.

-Liar

-Has an ex-girlfriend

who tried to ruin my

life when she had Will.

Imagine what'll happen

if I end up with him.

5 *To Be or Not to Be*

Jessica trudged up the Fowlers' steps, walked through the front door, and stared defeatedly at the gigantic tower of stairs leading up to the bedrooms.

Steps. Why did there have to be so many steps?

Working her entire shift at House of Java alongside Jeremy had required every ounce of strength she had inside her. Somehow, though, she had managed to make it through to the end without freaking out or bursting into tears again. Now if she could only reach the second landing and her queen-sized bed, she'd be in the clear.

Mustering up energy from her toenails and the tips of her eyelashes, she forced her weary body to mount each seven-inch rectangular rise of wood. Then she shuffled down the hallway to her room and collapsed on her bed, hugging one of her pillows to her chest. As the tension slowly seeped out of her, she finally let the tears she'd been holding in all day slip freely down her face.

There was only one word Jessica could think of to describe what Jeremy was doing to her, and it didn't gel with everything else she knew about him.

Cruel. He was being cruel to her for no reason. It was torture being in the same room with him and not being able to just kiss him or touch his shoulder or even hip-chuck him. It wasn't until that casual contact was taken away that she realized how truly close she and Jeremy had become. She felt like she was walking around with all her limbs tied to her body. She and Jeremy were like two mummies passing in the night.

There was no way she could go another four solid hours pretending Jeremy was just some coworker. If this went on much longer, she'd have to find another job. Something far less draining—like digging ditches.

He was testing her—seeing if she would run to Will. Well, she'd show him. From now on, she wouldn't even think about Will and his soft blond hair and big blue-gray eyes and musky aftershave smell. Nope. Will was out of her life. Completely.

The phone on her desk rang and Jessica's heart skipped a beat. Could it be Jeremy? Did he change his mind after that awkward work shift?

She grabbed the receiver, wiping her eyes with the back of her other hand. "Hello?" she said breathlessly.

"Jessica?" It was a guy. Not Jeremy.

"Yeah?" she replied.

"It's me. Will."

You have to be kidding me.

"Yes?" she said, her voice louder and colder.

"I was just calling to see how you were . . . I mean, after what happened Friday night. . . ."

He paused, waiting for a response, but Jessica didn't have one. She really didn't want to hear this. Not now. Why did he have to sound like that? Sympathetic. Sincere. She gripped the phone so hard, her fingers started to ache.

"I hope everything's okay," he continued, filling the silence. "I mean, he let you explain everything, right?"

"Yeah, sure," she mumbled. "I explained."

"Good. That's . . . great." His words said one thing, but his voice said another. Jessica detected a not-quite-hidden note of disappointment. *Why is he doing this? Why can't he just leave me alone?*

She had the sudden urge to tell him off, but she was simply too sapped to conjure up the anger.

"Look, Will," she said with a sigh, trying to make herself sound cool and indifferent. "I really . . . can't talk right now."

"Is something wrong?"

"Everything's fine. I . . . I just—"

"No. Something's up. Tell me what it is." His voice was low and his tone concerned. Jessica could feel the wall she'd constructed start to give.

"I . . . I have to go."

She started to put the receiver back down.

"Jessica."

Something about the way he said her name made her stop. His voice was soft and soothing—almost like a pillow. Jessica felt she could jump into the softness and cushion herself against everything she was going through. Slowly she raised the phone back up to her ear.

"What?" she asked weakly.

"Just tell me."

She blew out a long breath. "Fine. If you really want to know, Jeremy dumped me," she said.

"Why? You said you explained."

"I did," she said, her voice cracking. "But he thinks—"

Jessica stopped and swallowed hard. What was she doing? She couldn't tell Will that Jeremy thought she liked him. Was she insane?

"I guess he wants me to prove myself or something," she said numbly.

"How stupid is this guy?" Will asked. Jessica felt her heart lift slightly but squelched it. "I'm sorry, Jessica, but you deserve better than that."

Jessica smiled crookedly.

"So . . . are you gonna be okay?" Will asked, his tone full of warmth.

"Yeah. Thanks," she whispered. "I'll be fine." Nothing like a good ego boost to help her see things more clearly. Even if it was coming from a guy she'd just sworn to avoid like sour-cream-and-onion potato chips.

Will sighed slowly, and Jessica's face tingled as if he were breathing into her ear. "Listen, Jess. If there's anything I can do, just let me know. I mean it."

A warning buzzer went off in Jessica's brain as the tingling sensation faded away. This was dangerous territory.

"That's sweet, but . . . really, it's okay. Everything will work out," she declared, scraping up as much cheerfulness as possible to prove her point.

"Good," he said. "Well, anyway, I was also calling to ask about the kidnap. We still need to finish planning it."

"Oh, yeah," Jessica replied, bringing her free hand to her forehead. "I forgot about that."

"So, why don't you come over to my place on Tuesday after practice?" Will suggested.

Jessica went rigid. "Your house?"

Bad idea. Bad, bad, bad idea. The last time they'd sat down next to each other to "work," there had been all this laughing and touching and whispering. . . .

"Fine," she heard herself say. She closed her eyes. *You're nuts.* "I'll be there."

"Good," he said.

"I'll call Tia and let her know the plan," she added quickly. *Okay, not completely nuts,* she thought. There was a long pause at the other end of the line. Jessica held her breath.

"Cool," Will said finally. "I'll see ya around six."

Jessica knew he'd been trying to get her alone, and she wasn't exactly sure how she felt about that. She flopped back on her bed and closed her eyes.

"At least you thought of Tia," she muttered to herself, taking a deep, calming breath. Tia would be the buffer zone, just like she should have been the last time. And at this point, Jessica had to admit to herself, she needed that buffer zone.

Because Will Simmons could definitely be a lot more comforting than her pillow.

Ken scanned the library quickly, and the minute his eyes fell on Maria's soft, black curls, his dream came back to him in a hazy rush.

Should I tell her about it? he wondered as he crossed the room toward her. She looked up and smiled her hundred-watt smile as he approached, and he decided to keep his mouth shut. Knowing she had appeared in his dream was already making his nervous system go haywire. No reason to mess with hers too.

"Hey," he said, slipping into the heavy wooden chair across from her.

"Hey, you. Ready for the big exam?" she asked, her dark brown eyes sparkling.

"Let's see." He placed his fingers on his temples and shut his eyes in mock concentration. "That would be a no. Not by a long shot."

Maria rolled her eyes but kept right on smiling. "You did read the play, didn't you?"

"Yeah, I *read* it," he replied with a shrug. "It's *understanding* it that's the problem. The guy's always walking around talking to himself."

"Well, yeah," Maria whispered, shrugging out of her soft-looking purple cardigan. She was wearing a little, formfitting T-shirt underneath, and Ken averted his eyes to the surface of the table. "That's how the audience can know what Hamlet's thinking. See, the whole play is about his state of mind and how it changes."

"Action packed," Ken quipped, hazarding a glance up at her face.

"Yeah, I know. You'd probably think any story without a car-chase scene is a yawner." It was unbelievable how her smile lit up the entire room. "But it really is exciting," she said. "See, in the beginning Hamlet is totally depressed because of his dad's death and his mom remarrying his uncle Claudius. Listen."

Maria picked up her battered paperback copy of the play and opened it flat on the table. Then, in a stage whisper, she read:

"'O, that this too too solid flesh would melt,
Thaw and resolve itself into a dew!
Or that the Everlasting had not fix'd
His canon 'gainst self-slaughter! O God! God!
How weary, stale, flat and unprofitable
Seem to me all the uses of this world!'"

Hearing her add inflection and emotion to the same words he'd forced himself to read days before suddenly made the meaning a lot clearer. Not crystal clear, but close. Ken could almost picture Hamlet skulking around the castle, brooding. It reminded Ken of himself, the state of mind he was in at the start of school. After Olivia's death. Before Maria . . .

"Hear what I mean?" Maria asked. "He was too weirded out to do much of anything. And then he sees the ghost of his father, who tells him he was actually murdered. Suddenly Hamlet is spurred into taking some action, some type of vengeance, but he just doesn't know how."

Again Ken was reminded of his dream. Olivia had been sitting with Maria, both cheering him on, and Olivia had disappeared. Was that supposed to spur him into action? Was he supposed to be with Maria or something?

Nah. It was just a dream, not some Shakespearean ghost encounter. Besides, any quack psychologist could interpret its meaning. It only showed how much he missed the team and Olivia, and he was spending a lot of time with Maria. That was all.

A hand waved in front of his face.

"Hello-o? Ken? You still with me, or were you transported onto some thirty-yard line?"

Ken blushed. "How did you know I was thinking about football?"

"Oh, I have my ways," she replied, smirking.

"Whenever you think about playing, your eyes get all narrow and your face gets all serious. It makes me want to hike my shoe to you just to see if you'd automatically hurl it across the room."

"So I'm that pathetic, huh?" he said, leaning forward and rubbing his hands over his face.

Maria tilted her head and squinted at him thoughtfully. "You know, Ken. If football means that much to you, maybe you shouldn't give up so easily."

"What else am I supposed to do?" he asked. "I already tried storming the field. Coach Riley doesn't want me there."

"I don't know," Maria said, slumping back in her seat. "Maybe there's some other way to show him how serious you are."

"How? By hurling your shoe?" Ken asked with a laugh.

Maria suddenly sat up straight and pulled her chair right up to the table. "What if you just went up there and started running laps with the team or something?" she asked.

"I already tried going to practice," Ken whispered back. "He tossed me out."

"Yeah, but what if you'd just ignored him and stayed?" she asked, her eyes wide. "*That* would show him how dedicated you are, and what's he gonna do? Wrestle you off the field?"

Ken leaned back in his chair as he considered the image. What *would* Coach do? He'd probably freak out and yell until all the blood vessels in his face exploded. But even if he did spontaneously combust, he just might be impressed by Ken's never-say-die attitude.

"You know, Maria," he said in a distant, thoughtful voice. "You're either gonna get me killed or get me back on the team."

"Well, I can't wait to find out which," she replied. Her cheeks grew rosy as she grinned at him. "But in the meantime, will you please wipe off that quarterback expression and get back to the play? And I mean the *Shakespeare* play, not the quarterback sneak."

"I'll try," he said, returning the grin. "But you better watch your shoes just in case."

Tia stood on the Desmonds' front porch, trying to mortar a serene smile to her face before she knocked. No telling what she'd be facing once she got inside. Angel could still be zombified with despair, and his parents were probably in perpetual freak-out mode.

But looking calm and pleasant came easier now that she knew Conner was on the case. She was dying to tell Angel. Unfortunately, all last night Mr. Walker had been watching her like a sharpshooter until she left the club, so she hadn't been able to say anything then. Now she couldn't wait to be the bearer of good news. Angel definitely needed it. He might have said he didn't want her help, but she knew better. He was only being defensive.

Tia took a deep breath, mentally preparing herself, and rang the doorbell. Five seconds later the door opened—no, more like exploded inward—and Angel stood there, gazing at her with the widest grin she'd ever seen him wear. It was almost unnatural.

Her own fixed smile faded instantly.

"Hey!" he said, scooping her into his arms and half hugging, half dragging her through the doorway. "I'm so glad you're here!"

"Uh, yeah. Me too," she mumbled, narrowing her eyes at him. *Did I miss something? Did Conner already tell him the news and trash my big surprise?* "What's with the manic act?" she asked. "Did you get the money back or something?"

"Nope." Angel shook his head, touching her shoulder and then running his hand down her arm until he was holding her hand. "Come in my room a sec. There's something I want to tell you." He tugged on her hand, and Tia followed him, walking stiffly.

"Ookay," she said, her sneakers squeaking against the shiny hardwood steps. "I have something to tell you too." Although she wasn't sure her news could possibly make him happier than he already, inexplicably, was.

Angel sauntered into his room and shut the door behind them. For a moment he just stood there, grinning at her like an excited little kid.

"You first," he said, sticking his hands in the

72

pockets of his cargo shorts. "I'm a gentleman."

"Right." Tia shook her head slightly. "Okay, Conner had a brainstorm. You know how his mom is involved in all those charities? Well, he's going to get her to look into some scholarships for you! If she comes through, you are Stanford bound." She grinned at him, waiting for him to hug her or kiss her or at least react.

"Tell him not to bother," Angel said.

Not quite the reaction she was going for.

"Excuse me?" she asked, leveling him with an incredulous stare. "Anyone taken your temperature lately?"

Angel clapped. "Sit down, Tee," he said. "I have news."

Baffled, Tia just dropped onto the bed. Angel knelt beside her and grabbed her hands in his.

"All right. This is getting weird," she said, her heart pounding with an as-yet-unfounded concern. "Tell me what's going on."

Angel locked eyes with her and took a deep breath. "I've decided I'm not going, Tia," he blurted out. "Forget Stanford. I'm going to stay here with you."

A dozen conflicting thoughts jammed up inside Tia like speeding bumper cars. She wasn't sure whether to laugh, cry, throw something, or pinch herself to ensure that the moment wasn't just fabricated by her subconscious mind. Eventually she

73

caught her breath and dammed up the tide of rushing emotions.

"Explanation?" she asked.

"It just came to me," Angel said, all earnestness. He reached up and held her chin with his fingers. "This whole gambling thing happened for a reason. I was never meant to go to college. It's like fate's telling me what I should already know—that I'm supposed to be here with you."

Tia felt herself splintering and separating into several different Tias—like those Russian nesting dolls she used to play with when she was little. The outer Tia's face was frozen with shock. Just beneath that, a second Tia was in an all-out state of panic. And somewhere within her layers a version of her was smiling. Part of her, one of her, loved hearing the sweetness behind his words and the magnitude of his gesture. In a way, it was a dream come true.

But something wasn't right. Underneath it all, Tia was scared.

"You're insane!" she cried as the core of her feelings rushed to the surface. "You can't do this, Angel."

"Why not?" he said, getting up and sitting next to her. "My parents never went to college, and they're doing great. It just isn't in my blood. It wasn't meant to be."

"Are you even listening to yourself?" Tia leaped to her feet. She pushed her thick hair back from her face and held it there. "You worked so hard for that scholarship, and you've been slaving away for months to earn money for school. Why would *fate* or whatever you're talking about allow *that* to happen if it wasn't meant to be?"

He stood and faced her. "Because I was mixed up! I thought I wanted to go to Stanford, but now I know I don't." He took both her hands in his. "I know it sounds stupid and old-fashioned, but I don't even care," he said. "The gambling, losing my money, all of it happened for a purpose. To wake me up and make me realize I'm supposed to stay with you."

Tia's eyes filled with tears, and an angry helplessness welled up inside her. She pulled away her hands. "All this didn't happen for a higher purpose, Angel," she said flatly, her lip trembling. "It happened because you screwed up!"

A wounded expression passed over Angel's features and disappeared as quickly as it came. Then his face grew dark and steely, as if forming a shield to ward off further blows.

"Oh, really?" he muttered. "You might find it interesting to know this whole mess started with our big anniversary celebration. That's what I needed the money for in the first place. For *you*—not school."

Tia felt as if the love of her life had just trampled on her heart. "You can't blame this on me," she said, a tear spilling over. "I never cared what we did that night. You know that!"

He shrugged slightly and stared off toward the

wall. Tia wanted to scream at him for pinning his problems on her, but a tiny voice in the back of her mind reminded her that he was just looking for a scapegoat. And she wasn't going to let him have it.

"You're just giving up, Angel," Tia said, struggling to remain focused. "But you can't. You *have* to go to Stanford."

"I thought you'd be happy," Angel said accusingly, drawing away. "For some reason, I thought you loved me and wanted me to stay with you forever. Obviously I was wrong."

"I *do* love you, Angel. But—"

"Then why are you pushing me away?" he demanded. His eyes were large and liquid, and his voice had taken on a desperate edge. "You say I shouldn't work so hard at school and let it come to nothing, but what about us? What have I been putting in all this time with you for?"

His words hung in the air like a heavy, gray cloud.

Tia's heart sank into her stomach. "I thought it was because you loved me," she said weakly.

Angel just stared at the floor.

With a deep breath Tia somehow managed to lift her quavering chin. "But maybe *I* was wrong. If you've just been 'putting in time' to serve some end, then maybe I should let you out of your contract."

Angel glared back at her, his jaw rigid.

"This isn't about us, Angel," she went on, her

voice gaining strength. "It's about your future. Get your head out of the sand and deal with reality!"

"I'm not going!" he shouted. "I can't!"

As if to punctuate his meaning, Angel stalked over to his desk and swiped it clean, noisily knocking his clock, stapler, a dozen pens and pencils, and all his Stanford paperwork into the trash can. Tia stood there, hugging herself, as he walked out of the room and slammed the door.

This isn't happening, Tia told herself, trembling. *This is* not *happening.*

Eventually Tia's breathing returned to normal. Crossing the room, she carefully lifted the Stanford papers out of the can, tucked them under her arm, and walked out.

Angel might have decided to give up on his future, but she wasn't about to. Not by a long shot.

Jeremy Aames

An Open Letter to the Controlling Forces of the Universe

Dear . . . Whatever's Out There:

Enough already! Stop torturing me! I can't think of a single thing I've done to deserve it—unless you count stealing Trent's Chewbacca toy in kindergarten or breaking my grandmother's china platter when I was eight. I mean, come on! Do these crimes really merit the family's financial ruin? My dad's heart attack?

Jessica and Will?

Maybe I should have eaten all those lima beans I hid in my pockets when I was a kid.

Look, when I first met Jessica, she made things seem okay again. I thought, Hey, things are finally looking up. This is my guardian angel or whatever, sent directly to me to make things better. But instead she turned out to be a cruel joke. You put this beautiful, cool, smart, perfect girl in front of me and then said, "Ha! You can't have her!"

Are you somehow under the impression that I can handle all this? Because I can't.

So what I'm saying is, at some point—hopefully soon—I would really, really like a break. Please! I'm begging you! I'll find Chewbacca and give him back. I'll eat nothing but greens three meals a day. Just back off. Please. Okay. That's it.

Thank you for your time.
                    Jeremy Aames

P.S. If you need someone new to pick on, there's this guy named Will Simmons. . . .

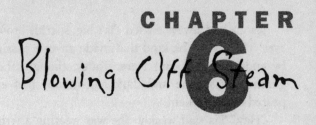

CHAPTER 6
Blowing Off Steam

"These early morning meetings should be outlawed," Jessica muttered as she made her way to the auditorium on Monday morning. After a night of nonsleep she wasn't even remotely up for a hyper drama club meeting. She'd considered skipping, but then she'd realized Tia would be there, and she wanted to talk to her friend about the meeting at Will's as soon as possible.

Tia had been at Angel's the night before when Jessica had called to ask her. Lucky girl. *It must be nice to have a guy like him,* Jessica thought. *To have that kind of security.*

Suddenly Jessica spotted Tia's glossy dark hair as she rounded the doorway to the auditorium.

"Tee!" she called out, hoping to grab her before she went inside. Once they entered Ms. Delaney's realm, the teacher-director would demand their utmost attention. Loudly.

Tia turned around slowly. The moment Jessica got a look at her friend's face, she forgot everything she was going to say.

Jessica had always envied Tia's big, sparkly brown eyes. They were the kind that made anyone passing by suddenly stop and stare. Today, though, their glimmer was gone and dark half-moons had appeared beneath them.

"Hey," Tia said weakly. She was wearing a wrinkled pink T-shirt and a pair of low-rider jeans. Not exactly her normal bright, put-together style.

"Are you okay?" Jessica asked.

Tia closed her eyes and wiped the back of her hand across her forehead. "Yeah. I'm fine. I just . . . haven't been sleeping well."

"I hope you aren't coming down with something," Jessica said, her brow creasing as a wave of panic washed through her. *If Tia's sick, she won't be able to meet me at Will's house. If she doesn't go to Will's, I'll end up alone with him. If I end up alone with him . . .*

"I'm okay," Tia replied at about half her normal amped-up volume. "I'm just dealing with some stuff with Angel."

Angel.

Selfish much, Jessica? she chided herself. There was obviously something huge going on, and all she could think about was her stupid Will problems. Some friend she was.

"What is it?" Jessica instinctively put her hand on Tia's arm. "What's going on?"

Tia glanced over her shoulder at the auditorium.

Most of the drama club was already gathered in the first couple of rows. "Can I tell you after the meeting?" she said softly.

"Sure," Jessica said, hugging her books to her chest. She hoped Tia and Angel hadn't broken up or something. Jessica's faith in true love would be forever tainted if the supercouple had called it quits.

"All right, everyone!" Ms. Delaney called, clapping as she walked out from the wings. "Let's all find some seats. We'll be getting down to business in just a moment."

Tia started inside, but Jessica grabbed her wrist.

"Listen, Tia," she whispered quickly. "This might not be a good time, but I have a favor to ask."

"What's up?" Tia asked, leaning back against the wall.

"Will wants us to come over to his house after cheerleading practice tomorrow to finish planning the kidnap," Jessica explained quickly. "Can you come?"

She glanced over Tia's shoulder at the stage, hoping Delaney hadn't noticed them yet. Luckily she was busy talking with Renee Talbot.

"I don't know, Jess," Tia muttered.

"Listen, I don't know what's going on with you and Angel," Jessica said, "but maybe this will help you take your mind off it for a little while."

Tia eyed her skeptically, so Jessica decided to go

for the bluntly honest approach. "Besides, I can't go by myself."

Tia's brow furrowed. "Because of Will?"

"Yeah, sort of," she said feebly. "Jeremy saw me with Will on Friday night and broke up with me."

"Oh, God. I'm so sorry!" Tia's sunken eyes filled with pity. Then realization seemed to sweep over her features. "Oh, no. If I had been there—"

"No!" Jessica said. "It's not your fault at all. It's not like you could have known. But the point is, I cannot be alone with Will. I have to get Jeremy back, and if he finds out—"

Tia sighed and crossed her arms in front of her chest. "Are you afraid he'll find out, or are you afraid you might do something with Will?"

Jessica felt her face turn bright red, and she trained her eyes on the floor.

"You know what?" Tia said, pushing away from the wall. "It doesn't matter. I'll be there."

"That's great!" Jessica exclaimed.

"It's the least I can do," Tia said somberly.

Jessica hugged Tia, barely containing herself from bouncing up and down. "You're saving my life," she said.

Tia grunted a laugh. "I wouldn't go that far."

"Girls?" Ms. Delaney called out to them. "Would you mind sitting down and joining the rest of us?"

Jessica rolled her eyes at Tia, and they made their way down the aisle, plopping into two open seats at the back of the crowd.

"Just tell me," Jessica whispered as Tia pulled out a notebook from her messenger bag. "Is this thing with Angel fixable?"

Tia stared at her hands. "I don't know," she said quietly. "I really don't."

"Man, am I glad you asked me to meet you here, Conner," Angel mumbled to his coffee mug. "I was going crazy at home."

"The feeling's mutual," Conner said.

Angel sighed and stared out the front window of House of Java. Funny. He used to love getting a day off from his dad's garage now and then. It made him feel so . . . free. But today had been different. Today was no holiday.

Angel had spent the entire day lying around, watching soap operas and feeling sorry for himself. He'd never thought he'd miss that loud, fumy garage, but he did. And he missed hanging around with his dad too. It had been days since his father looked him in the eye.

"I figured you could use a break," Conner said, taking a gulp of his black-as-pitch coffee.

Angel snorted. "Break from what? When you called me from school, I was watching a rerun of *Matlock*."

Conner smirked. "You're right. You should be thanking me."

"Man, I'm so lame," Angel muttered, leaning

85

forward and resting his head in his hands. "Fired by my own father. Watching geriatric television. And right now this cup of coffee is all I can afford."

Conner sat there, slouched back in his chair, and watched Angel silently. Angel was glad he didn't offer words of condolence. Pity was the last thing he needed right now.

Angel shook his head, sitting back, almost mimicking Conner's casual posture. "Even Tia thinks I'm lame."

"No, she doesn't," Conner said.

"Didn't she tell you what happened?" Angel asked.

Conner shrugged slightly. "I didn't see much of her today."

"Well, you should've seen her last night," Angel countered, sitting up again. Apparently he couldn't do the bad-posture thing. "Man, I had it all worked out. It was supposed to be beautiful. I sat her down and told her I'd decided not to go to college and that I was going to stay and be with her, but she—"

Conner put down his coffee cup with an unusually resonant bang. "*What* did you tell her?"

"I told her the reason I lost all my savings was because I was meant to. I'm supposed to be with her, Conner. I know it." He sighed and absently twisted his coffee mug around. "But I guess I'm not good enough for her now. She wasn't the least bit happy. All she could do was keep telling me how wrong I was and how I messed up big time."

"Hey, Angel," Conner began, sitting up and leaning his elbows on the table. He pinched the top of his nose and sighed, then finally looked Angel in the eye. "I know that Tia has this habit of exaggerated reaction, but this time she's right."

Angel's mouth dropped open. Conner couldn't have shocked him more if he'd thrown his drink in his face. Since when did Conner judge anything anyone did?

"I'm sorry, man," Conner said. "But if you don't—"

"You know, if you'd actually think about my side of things instead of getting on my case, you'd realize there is no way out!" Angel barked.

Conner's green eyes flashed. "Chill, man. I'm just calling it like I see it," he said.

"Oh, yeah? Well, don't do me any favors," Angel grumbled.

Conner sighed and ran his hands through his shaggy hair, scratching at the back of his neck.

"I guess you'll like this news," Conner said.

"What?" Angel asked.

"My mom looked into those club handouts, but it doesn't look good," Conner said. "They only give out their scholarships at the end of the school year. I mean, there's still a shot, but I just wanted to let you know."

A boiling mixture of shame and anger coursed

through Angel's veins at the thought of Mrs. Sandborn begging for him. How low could he sink?

"I don't know why you even bothered," Angel snapped. "I never asked for any charity."

"It's called *friendship*," Conner said, slowly drawing out the pronunciation. "Look it up."

"Just drop it," Angel muttered. "It's done. I'm staying behind whether you guys like it or not." He glared down at the tabletop.

Out of the corner of his eye Angel saw Conner shake his head in frustration. What would the next lecture be? The snap-out-of-it speech? Or the don't-give-up-hope speech?

"Whatever, man," Conner said as he stood up. "I think you're an idiot, but it's your life." He dropped a few crumpled bills on the table. "Later." Then he turned and casually strolled out of the café.

Angel stared after him, dumbfounded. *What? No more slams? No more words of advice?* Had he actually been spared another pep talk?

Finally! Someone was going to back off and let him make his own decisions. He should feel relieved. He should bow his head in gratitude. He should celebrate with another coffee!

But Angel's heart was unexpectedly heavy as he stared at Conner's empty chair. For some reason, the fact that Conner had given in so easily made Angel feel oddly betrayed.

* * *

Tia stretched her arms out and behind her, cracking her back loudly.

Somehow she had made it through a drama-club meeting; a lengthy venting session with Jessica; seven yawn-inducing classes; an endless lunch with Andy, who attempted various scientific experiments with his onion rings; and a one-hour work session in the gym, finishing up spirit posters with the rest of the cheerleaders. She'd even stayed late by herself to clean up after everyone. And now her hours of school torture were finally over. Unfortunately, she still had to face the rest of her miserable existence.

"But first, a shower," she said aloud, scratching at the thick dabs of paint drying on her skin. A particularly large, itchy green patch covered her left knee. It would probably take a sandblaster to get that one off.

A strange feeling of déjà vu settled over Tia as she walked through the silent hall. The sensation of paint on skin, the smell of the fumes, the weird splashes of color on her legs and arms. It all reminded her of something. . . .

The tree house.

Tia giggled, shaking her head. Two summers ago Angel had suddenly decided to build a fort for her brothers in the backyard. For three straight days they sawed, hammered, and nailed various-sized planks across the giant limbs of their oak tree. And on the fourth day they painted—the walls, floor, roof, and each other. In the end, it was a ramshackle structure that actually resembled a giant wooden cage more than a house.

She smiled as she remembered herself and Angel laughing and flinging their paintbrushes at each other, causing sprays of red color to shoot out like bullets. By the end of the skirmish they both looked like a couple of giant Elmo dolls. And when he'd cupped her face in his hands and kissed her, she'd wound up with two scarlet streaks on each cheek. It took ten full minutes to convince her mother she wasn't bleeding—and another four days to get the paint out of her hair.

Why can't life be like that? she wondered glumly. *Why can't we just wash off the stuff we don't want to last?* But this whole gambling episode had left Angel genuinely wounded—not just paint smeared. And she had a feeling it would take months for the damage to fade. If ever.

"Hey, Tia."

Tia blinked hard and shook her head, erasing her mind like an Etch-A-Sketch pad. She looked up to find Elizabeth trudging toward her. "Oh. Hey, Liz. Where did you come from?"

"Oracle," Elizabeth said, gesturing over her shoulder.

"What's up?" Tia asked, eyeing her friend warily. She looked like she'd just woken up, and it was four-thirty in the afternoon.

Elizabeth shrugged indifferently and sighed. "Not much."

It pained Tia to look at her. The Elizabeth she had gotten to know at the beginning of the school year—the happy, confident ray of sunshine—was nowhere to be found. The impostor in front of her resembled that Elizabeth in every way, except the spark was gone. Like a candle someone had blown out. And that someone, she knew, was her randomly callous buddy, Conner McDermott.

It seemed like no one was having an easy time of it lately.

"I was wondering . . . ," Elizabeth began, nervously twirling a lock of hair between her fingers. "Are you going to hang out at the Riot tonight and visit Angel?"

Tia's heart stung, like an old sore suddenly reopened. "Uh . . . probably not." She was about to tell Elizabeth the whole story but thought the better of it. She didn't want to go over all the gory details again, and Elizabeth definitely didn't look like she was in the mood to hear them. "That manager of his is a real jerk, and I don't want to be a distraction. Besides, I'm pretty beat."

"Oh, okay," Elizabeth said, looking at the floor. "Do you think maybe Andy and the guys might go?"

She was trying to sound nonchalant and failing miserably. Tia could interpret the real question, the one Elizabeth's eyes asked. *Is Conner going to be there?*

"I really don't know what the guys are up to," Tia replied, trying to keep the pity out of her voice and expression. "But since this is usually a dead night, I'd say no."

Elizabeth's face drooped dejectedly. It was more than Tia could bear. Jessica was panicked, Elizabeth was the personification of despair, and Tia didn't know which way was up. All because of the idiot guys in their lives.

Suddenly she had an idea. An idea that made her feel like herself for the first time all day.

"Brainstorm!" she said with a smile. "Why don't you, me, Jessica, and Maria get together after the game on Saturday and have a girls' night? You know, just watch videos and consume way too many calories?"

"Yeah, sure," Elizabeth replied unenthusiastically. "Not like I have anything else to do."

"Cool! It'll be like an old-fashioned girl party." *Just what we all need,* Tia added silently.

Elizabeth forced a smile. "Okay. That could be cool. Well . . . I'll see ya later."

"Later," Tia called as she watched Elizabeth's hunched shoulders disappear around the corner.

"Back pat!" Tia said to herself, patting behind her shoulder. She was going to get her friends' minds off love and testosterone if it killed her. She turned and pulled open the locker-room door, but suddenly she froze.

If Angel went to Stanford, Tia was going to have to start getting used to girls' nights.

If he went.

Tia hung her head and trudged into the locker room, dejected all over again. If only she could shut off her brain.

Conner strummed an E chord on his acoustic guitar and let it hang in the air of his bedroom. He was getting that feeling. That restless itch that always inspired him to compose songs.

He certainly had his pick of topics. He could knock off a twangy country song about his family situation. "Mama's on the Wagon, but the Wagon Ain't Rollin'"? A cynical love ballad on his social life. "Kicked to the Curb." Or how about a blues tune about his buddy in money trouble? "Angel Lost His Wings."

Conner sighed and shook his head. He was definitely losing it.

Unfortunately, there was nothing he could do about his problems *but* write a song. It wasn't like he could change things.

Conner took a deep breath and blew it out slowly, thinking about Angel's little act at the coffeehouse. He could tell by the look on Angel's face that he had expected Conner to try to talk him into going to college. But why bother? Why play the role of someone's conscience? It never did any good.

If there was one thing Conner had learned, it was that no one changed unless they wanted to. Their family and friends could nag until they were gasping for oxygen, but if they didn't want to do something, they wouldn't. Conner felt sorry for Angel, and he really hoped the country-club snobs would come through with a scholarship, but otherwise he couldn't help him. The guy had to realize that when you messed up, you had to pay the consequences. Nothing came easy.

Conner picked out a series of notes and cleared his throat. "Everyone's searching for a quick solution . . . ," he sang.

Why did people always look for a fast track to solving their problems? Angel let himself believe that there was a shortcut to making money. He thought gambling was the quick, easy way out. What he didn't realize was that *life* was a gamble. Everything— health, relationships, the possibility of getting crushed in an earthquake—everything already hinged on chance. But people still wanted to believe they could cheat the system.

Like Elizabeth. She thought she could just smile her perfect smile and all of Conner's problems would magically disappear. She had no clue what real life was all about. Sometimes you just had to accept the hand you were dealt.

"Wake up, world. Life's never easy," he sang, trying a new chord.

Suddenly a loud clatter sounded from downstairs. Conner stopped midstrum. It was probably his mom getting back from wherever she'd gone. Conner strained to hear her footsteps coming up the stairs. Hmmm. Sounded like a regular rhythm. Maybe she hadn't gone drinking after all.

He opened the door just as his mother stepped onto the second-story landing. Her movements seemed natural, and her makeup and outfit still looked in order. She turned toward him and smiled.

"Hi, honey. How was school?"

"Where have you been?"

She narrowed her eyes. "Out having coffee with some friends. Is that okay with you?"

Conner gave a quick nod. "Fine."

"Good," she exclaimed, raising her chin disdainfully. "Any more questions?"

"Just one. How's the Angel thing? Hear anything new?"

His mother sighed and shook her head. "Conner, I told you that would take some time."

"He doesn't have time," Conner said, gripping the doorknob.

"Don't worry," his mother said reassuringly. "I promise you I'm doing what I can. Now, I have another meeting this Saturday with the Sacred Heart Foundation people. They'll probably be our best bet, so just be patient."

Conner scrutinized her face for a moment,

searching for a crack in the "dutiful mother" mask she was wearing. But he found nothing. Just total sincerity.

Something's up, he thought. *Things are never this easy. At least not around here.*

"Well, if it's all right with you, I'm off to bed." She turned and headed down the hallway. A few steps from her door she stopped and glanced back at him. "Oh, and Conner? Please tell Angel to hang in there. I'll know everything by Saturday."

Conner frowned as his mother walked into her bedroom. He was about to warn her not to blow it but stopped himself at the last second. No sense making her mad. As long as she was possessed by this Mrs. Brady spirit, Angel at least had half a chance.

Could she actually come through for them? Could she actually be cleaning up her act?

Don't go there, he thought, trampling all traces of optimism as he went back into his room and closed the door.

Knowing his mom, Angel's odds at the track were probably better.

Conner McDermott

<u>Song notes</u>

Got to get out of this place.

Got nowhere to go, no open space.

Everyone's running, no clue, no hope . . .

hope

rope

nope

lope

mope

slope

the end of our rope . . .

it's a slippery slope . . .

This is pathetic.

CHAPTER 7
Into the Lion's Den

Taking a deep breath, Ken pushed through the locker-room doors and casually jogged out to the football field.

Just play it cool, he told himself, even though he couldn't stop his knees from shaking as he approached the team. *If Coach loses it, ignore him. This is where you belong, whether he likes it or not.*

Ken could hear the other guys grow quiet as he came closer. He scanned the field and noted that Coach hadn't come out to start practice yet. A low murmur reverberated through the crowd like a crashing wave. The reactions, as he'd expected, were mixed.

"All right, Matthews!" Todd called out.

"Yeah, man!" Bruce Covington shouted.

Other members of his former offensive line slapped him on the back, offering encouraging words. Ken felt as though he'd come home after a long trip. Then he noticed a group of El Carro diehards crowding around Will Simmons, all giving Ken the death eye.

"What the hell are you doing here?" a meaty-faced lineman snarled.

"Yeah. Go join some team that wants you," Josh Radinsky spat, earning a round of affirmative grunts from his sidekicks.

Will stepped forward and held up his hand, turning to face his teammates. "Hey, if Matthews wants to try the field and take a few patented El Carro tackles, that's his business. I'm sure he'll just up and quit again when he feels like it."

Ken clenched his jaw to keep from cutting the guy down. He was here to join the team, not divide it.

At that moment Coach Riley marched onto the field and blew his whistle. "All right, men! Ten laps around! Move like a lion's on your butt. Now go!"

Coach whistled again, and the team, after hesitating a second to glance from Coach to Ken and back again, raced off. Ken ran with them, hanging a little to the back. He knew Coach hadn't seen him yet and hoped to take advantage of that as long as he could. Besides, he was a little out of shape and needed to pace himself.

His luck lasted for two and a half laps. Then, just as he was hitting a good stride, he heard Coach bellow, "Matthews! What the hell do you think you're doing?"

"Running laps, Coach," he replied breathlessly.

"Get lost!" Coach Riley yelled. "Now!"

Ken simply shook his head as he ran. By now he was rounding the corner and coming toward Coach's position on the sidelines.

Riley's skin was as red as the SVH windbreaker he was wearing. "Matthews! You get your butt out of here before I haul it off the field myself!"

"Sorry, Coach," he said, grateful he didn't have to yell to be heard. "I guess you'll just have to haul me off."

As he rounded the next corner, Ken sneaked a sideways glance and saw Coach Riley angrily pacing up and down the sidelines, clenching his fists and shouting at the top of his lungs.

"You think this is funny?" he yelled. "You think this is some sort of game? Do I look like I'm amused?"

Ken just kept on running. A few of the other guys muttered their own comments—the SVH guys egging him on and the El Carro loyalists adding threats of their own. Ken responded to none of it, focusing instead on the rhythm of his jog.

The next time he came into range, he heard Coach ranting, ". . . is a football team! Not some damn merry-go-round you can hop onto whenever you feel like it! You think just because . . ."

Ken knew that making Riley mad was never a good idea, but he'd been left with no choice. At least now Coach, and the team, would know how serious he was about playing. As he finished his tenth lap, he slowed with the rest of the team in front of the coach. The players glanced expectantly from Ken to Coach Riley, salivating for the outcome of the duel.

"Men, as you might have noticed, we have a former member who thinks he can jump back in after skipping out on all our hard work these past few weeks," Coach said, hands on hips. "Now I, personally, don't think that's fair."

A few of Will's henchmen grunted in agreement.

"However, if this meathead wants to waste his energy practicing with you, that's his business."

The SVH guys nodded and nudged one another.

"But understand this, Matthews," Coach hissed, staring directly at Ken. "This doesn't mean you're back on the team. It doesn't mean anything, as far as I can tell. Except that you're a class-A moron."

Ken resisted the urge to smile. At least he had permission to work out with the team. He'd take each victory as it came—large or small.

"Now, ladies!" Coach said, addressing the team. "Your pass plays were sorry on Saturday. My grandma could have run a better pattern with her sewing machine! So today we are going to run those plays. And we'll run 'em and run 'em and run 'em until you're running 'em in your sleep. You got that?"

"Yes! Coach!" the team responded.

"Let's go!" Coach blew his whistle, and the team broke into opposing sides. Ken hesitated, debating whether he should huddle up with the offense. With

Simmons calling the shots, there was really no place for him.

"Hey, Ken," Todd said. "Take my place as receiver, and I'll sit the next few plays out."

Ken smiled gratefully. "Thanks, man."

"No problem. Good luck." Todd punched him lightly on the shoulder and jogged over to the sidelines.

As Ken crouched into the huddle, Will sneered at him blatantly.

"Okay, Matthews. I know it's been a while since you've seen any action, and you don't know squat about our new offense," he said. "So do us a favor and just stay out of our way." Then he called out a play, clapped his palms, and broke the huddle.

Ken headed to the line and fought to keep a straight face when he saw his opponent. The El Carro defenders had managed to line up Amos Kavanaugh, the new Godzilla-sized cornerback, opposite him.

"I'm gonna be all over you," Kavanaugh grunted as they squatted down face-to-face. "I'm gonna be on you like a blanket. No way you're gonna see the ball this practice."

Will snapped the ball, and before Ken could even blink, Kavanaugh's two-hundred-pound frame barreled into him, flattening him into the solid ground.

"Aww, whatsamatter?" Kavanaugh chided, pacing

at Ken's feet as Ken lay stunned on his back, struggling for breath. "Is this too rough for you? Maybe you should quit and go back to being the burnout that you are."

Ken could hear the others laugh and slap hands. But the words just rolled off him. He didn't even mind the throbbing in his sides or the blood in his mouth. In fact, he suddenly felt very much alive. After months of walking around numb and aloof, it was good to actually feel this strongly about something again—even if that feeling was searing pain.

"You all right?" Todd asked, coming off the sidelines to help pull him to his feet. Ken could read the pity in his eyes.

"Fine," Ken replied. "Ready for more."

"You know"—Todd lowered his voice—"if you aren't up for this, it's okay. I mean, no one will blame you for giving in. Maybe after you've learned the new calls and—"

"No!" Ken snapped. "I can *do* this. I know where I need to be—I just have to get past Kavanaugh."

Todd nodded. "All right. Let me tell you something about Kavanaugh. When he plays bump and run, his first move is always to the right. If you go left, you're home free."

"Thanks, man," Ken replied with a grin. "That's just what I need."

Will was smiling smugly when Ken returned to the huddle. *Yeah, go ahead and get cocky,* Ken thought. *I'm not in this for glory anymore. I'm in it for my own survival.*

Ken recognized the pass Will called. It was a simple crossing pattern, one Ken had thrown hundreds of times before.

He lined up with the others and ignored Kavanaugh's whispered threats. Then, when the ball was snapped, he quickly cut to Kavanaugh's left and sped to the designated spot before the appointed receiver could make it. Will, reacting to the sight of a helmet, launched the pass on cue. And Ken caught it easily.

Even the four defenders who flattened him from each direction couldn't knock the joy out of him.

Todd and a few others helped unearth him from the El Carro pileup.

"Not bad, Matthews," Todd said, slapping Ken's shoulder. "For a QB."

"Thanks, man," Ken said, tossing Todd the ball.

As the rest of the team ran back to the huddle, Ken glanced up into the stands where Olivia had been sitting in his dream and smiled.

"Okay, here's the plan," Jessica mumbled to herself as she drove into the south-side neighborhood, searching for Will's street. "First of all, I'm going to sit as far away from him as I can."

She located Gable Road and made a left.

"And I won't mention Jeremy at all. Or if I do, it

will be to talk about how unbelievably amazing he is."

She found Cliffwood Lane and made a right.

"And no matter what, no matter how sweet he tries to act or sympathetic he sounds, I won't let him get to me."

And there it was, 1143 Cliffwood. Will's house.

It even looks like Will, Jessica thought as she pulled into the driveway. The house had a cool, light beige brick exterior with blue trim and a row of thorny-looking, flowering bushes around the front. It was charming—in a strong, guarded sort of way.

She parked the Jeep right behind Will's Chevy Blazer. No turning back now.

"Just get it over with, Jess," she said, nervously drumming her fingers on the steering wheel. "You're only doing this for the school, to make sure the kidnap tradition goes off well. That's all."

After a studious glance in the rearview mirror, she jumped out of the Jeep, strolled up to the front door, and rang the doorbell. A full minute passed, and no one answered. She pushed the doorbell again. Still no response.

He is *here, isn't he?* she wondered, glancing over her shoulder at the parked Blazer. *Maybe the doorbell is busted?*

Jessica had raised her hand to rap on the door when it suddenly swung open. Her knuckles almost collided with Will's chest—his *bare* chest.

Her hand and jaw dropped simultaneously as

she took in the sight before her: Will wearing nothing but a pair of jeans . . . droplets of water glistening on his muscles . . . his hair damp from a recent shower . . . meaning just moments before he'd probably been wearing nothing at all. . . .

"Sorry. I'm running late," she heard him say. "Football practice was kind of weird today. It took longer than usual."

It occurred to her that she should make eye contact. "Oh . . . yeah," she squeaked, forcing herself to meet his gaze. "That's okay."

"I'm glad you could come," he said softly, the corners of his mouth lifting just enough to reveal his dimples.

Jessica quickly looked away to curb the swooning sensation in her legs. "Uh, sure—no problem," she stammered, concentrating on the clouds drifting overhead, the bark on a nearby tree, the geraniums in the clay pot near her feet. *Get a grip!* she scolded herself. *If you can't handle the first few seconds, how are you going to get through the evening?*

"Well, come on in. Tia's not here yet, but we can go ahead and get to work." He stepped back and held the door open for her.

Work! Yes! That was what she had to focus on. "Right," she replied, nodding. "We should get started."

As she passed by him, she could smell his intoxicating scent of shampoo and musky deodorant. And she couldn't help but notice the wet sheen on his arm muscles as he held the door ajar.

Stop it! she commanded herself as she hurried into the carpeted foyer.

A second later Jessica heard the front door shut behind her. So here she was. No turning back now. The rest of the house seemed empty, and a slight panicky sensation fluttered in her chest.

Me and Will. Will and me. Alone. In his house.

She mindlessly followed Will down a nearby hall.

"Come on in," Will said, gesturing toward a doorway she assumed led to his bedroom. "Sorry about the mess."

And there it was. Will's room. As self-conscious as she was about being there, she also couldn't help but be a little curious too. She'd always thought people's bedrooms revealed a lot about them.

The first thing she noticed was that despite Will's apology, it wasn't all that messy. There was a measure of clutter that someone like Elizabeth would dub a "mess," but not compared to Jessica's own standards of clean—or lack of standards, as it were. He had a double bed covered with a cushiony navy blue comforter, a desk strewn with papers, a long shelf crammed full of CDs and old *Sports Illustrated* magazines, and an assortment of sports paraphernalia (football, Frisbee, a couple of yo-yos) scattered about the beige carpeting. The only decorative objects in the room were a few framed photos and a poster of Troy Aikman on the closet door.

And everything about the room—from its contents to its cozy earth tones to the slight warmth in the air—positively screamed "Will."

"Grab a seat," he said, gesturing at his desk chair. "I'm going to throw on a shirt."

Jessica sat down and quickly scanned the nearby photographs in order to avoid staring at him while he changed. It surprised her that there were no pictures of Melissa or any evidence of her at all in the room. Jessica allowed herself a small, triumphant smile. What would Melissa think if she knew where Jessica was right now?

She wiped the smile off her face and pushed the feeling aside, concentrating on the photos.

There was a shot of two people who had to be Will's parents, a group photo of last year's El Carro football team, and one of a small boy.

She picked up the snapshot of the boy. He looked to be no more than ten years old, with bright yellow hair, freckles, and a row of giant white teeth poking out of his mouth like picket fence posts. The huge grin probably had something to do with the shiny gold baseball trophy he held above his head.

Will turned around and caught her staring at the picture. "Don't look at that," he said, wincing.

"Is this you?" Jessica asked.

He nodded and rolled his eyes. "Yeah. Before

puberty and a couple of thousand dollars' worth of orthodontics."

Glancing back at the picture, Jessica couldn't believe she hadn't noticed it before. She'd recognize those eyes anywhere.

But that smile! She'd never, ever seen the older Will look this happy. Usually he wore a cool, wary expression, and even his smiles didn't expose much emotion. Not the boy in the photo, though. He had an all-out, open-to-the-world happiness that warmed Jessica's heart. She wondered if those feelings still ran through Will on some subterranean level.

"I think it's a great shot," Jessica remarked. "Why do you have it out if you hate it so much?"

"It was taken on the best day of my life," he said, slipping an arm into a white oxford. "I know it sounds lame, but I still keep it around as sort of a good-luck charm."

Jessica smiled and set it back down. "It doesn't sound lame," she remarked. "I've got stuff like that too."

She leaned over and inspected Will's CD collection. Surprisingly, many of the titles were the same ones she had at home. But she reminded herself that it didn't mean anything. Probably two-thirds of the local population had the exact same tastes.

As she flipped her index finger through the stack, she suddenly came upon a familiar-looking gold-colored CD case.

"I don't believe it!" she exclaimed. *"Frank Sinatra's Greatest Hits!"*

"Uh . . . yeah," Will said sheepishly. "I like it 'cause it helps me relax. But don't tell anyone, or I'll have to live with some totally creative nickname like 'Softheart Simmons' for the rest of my life."

"I know!" Jessica nodded. "I used to really get into this old Sinatra record my dad had until Lila caught me listening to it once and laughed herself off the edge of my bed."

"Man, people just have no taste, huh?" he said with a wry grin. By now his shirt was buttoned up and neatly tucked into his jeans, so it was easier for Jessica to make visual contact.

This isn't so bad, she congratulated herself. It amazed her how different Will seemed now compared to when he was with Melissa. Had he changed? Or was this the real Will she just wasn't able to see before?

He walked over and took the CD from Jessica's grasp. "Let's play some music."

Will popped the disk into the stereo and adjusted the volume. Soon the tinkling of piano keys filled the air and Sinatra's voice began crooning, "I've got you under my skin. . . ."

Jessica laughed and shook her head.

"What?" he asked.

"Oh, nothing," Jessica replied. "I was just thinking about my dad. This is one of his all-time favorite

111

songs. Whenever he put on this album, he'd always pull me into the room and dance with me."

Jessica felt her face fall. Her dad's records had all been smashed in the quake. It had been a long time since she and her father had danced to anything.

"Shall we?" Will said in a comically deep voice.

"What?" Jessica asked.

Before she could even catch her breath, Will grabbed her hands and pulled her to her feet. Jessica stared at him, totally confused, and noticed a mischievous glint in his eyes. She smiled inadvertently, and Will wrapped his arms around her, waltzing her backward.

Jessica giggled with surprise as the room swirled. They tripped over the football and burst out laughing, but they didn't stop dancing. As Jessica's giggling subsided, Will looked into her eyes. Suddenly the playful dance slowed into an easy, rhythmic swaying.

Jessica closed her eyes and relaxed into the moment. Will's strong arms made her feel safe and cozy, and as he hummed along right next to her ear, the sound vibrations caused a tingling sensation all the way down her body. She took a deep breath and was surprised when it caught in her throat.

Will pulled his face back slightly, still holding her close.

She pulled back too and met his eyes. Then her gaze traveled slowly down to his soft, perfect lips. They were moving closer.

Jessica was being pulled into his space, and she was unable—unwilling—to break away. Nothing mattered. All she wanted was to feel his lips on hers. It had been so long.

Then, just as her eyes were fluttering closed in anticipation, Jessica heard a noise behind her. She jumped back, startled.

Tia stood in the doorway. Her eyebrows were raised, and her mouth was twisted into an amused smirk. "Am I interrupting something?"

This is interesting, Tia thought.

Jessica moved so far from Will so quickly, Tia was wondering if he was about to explode or something.

"Tia!" Jessica greeted her a little too animatedly. "Uh . . . Will and I were just messing around." She laughed awkwardly, and her eyes were pleading.

Tia flashed a dubious smile. Jessica and Will dancing, huh? Hmmm. She'd hoped this meeting would help take her mind off Angel's problems, but this was more than she'd bargained for. No wonder they hadn't heard the doorbell. Probably too distracted with the sweet nothings they were whispering to each other.

"Come on in, Tia," Will said, picking up a pile of clothes from his desk chair and placing them on top of the dresser. He crossed over to the CD player and clicked off the awful music they had been dancing to. The silence was beyond awkward.

"Thanks," Tia said, stepping out of the doorway. She studied Will's expression closely. While Jessica looked weak and shaky, Will seemed surprisingly calm. A little disappointed, maybe, but not nervous or guilty. What exactly was happening here? She'd thought Jessica needed her here so that things wouldn't be awkward with Will. But it seemed her showing up had *made* things awkward.

"So . . ." Jessica clapped. "Let's do this."

She started to sit down on the bed and sprang away, obviously thinking the better of it. Then she dropped down onto the floor, cross-legged, and Tia and Will followed her lead. Jessica nervously bounced her left knee and fiddled with the threads in the carpet. For a moment no one spoke.

"Sorry about missing the last meeting," Tia said, hoping to break the tense silence. "So what exactly is this kidnap thing we're organizing?"

"All right," Jessica said, leaning back on her hands. "It sounds weird, but what we do is go around to the cheerleaders' and football players' houses really early one morning, get them out of bed, and kidnap them. We don't give them time to change or do their hair or anything. Then we all go out for breakfast."

"Are you kidding me?" Tia exclaimed. "I don't even want to know the things you've seen."

"I do," Will said, grinning. "Dish the dirt. Like who sleeps with a teddy bear? Or wears Winnie-the-Pooh pajamas? Got any good stories?"

"Tons!" Jessica laughed, visibly relaxing. "Like when Ken ripped the blankets off Max Waters and he was completely naked."

"Completely?" Tia asked, her jaw dropping.

"One hundred percent raw," Jessica answered with a nod.

"What did he do?" Will asked, stunned.

"Screamed like a baby," Jessica said gleefully. "Can you imagine waking up to find the entire cheerleading squad running out of your bedroom screeching?"

Tia shook her head. "If anyone shows up to do that to me, I'll have my dad chase them off with his hunting rifle."

"Well, that's why we get the parents in on it," Jessica said. "We call them up ahead of time and explain the tradition. Oddly, none of them have ever had a problem with it."

"Okay. So let's plan this thing," Tia exclaimed. "Where do we start?"

Jessica briefly filled Tia and Will in on the details. All they needed to do was call up all the parents, find some reliable people to drive, and then divide up the list of "victims" among the drivers. Tia offered to call the parents of the cheerleaders, and Jessica and Will decided to split up calling the football players' parents. Then Jessica made out a list of everyone they had to kidnap, trying to figure out how many cars they would need to shuttle everyone around.

"I can fit five or six people in my car," Will said.

"I can stuff about five in the Jeep," Jessica added.

Tia twisted a lock of hair around her finger. "I could probably borrow my parents' minivan that day. It can hold maybe seven, if they aren't big linebackers or anything."

"We should have three more drivers to be safe," Jessica suggested. "But they have to be people we trust to keep their mouths shut."

"I can get a couple of guys," Will offered.

"And I bet Annie Whitman will do it," Tia said.

"Cool. That should be enough," Jessica said. "If we need more cars, we'll get some of the victims to drive as we go along."

"Great!" Tia exclaimed. "This is going to be so much fun. I can't wait to find out if Matt Wells wears boxers or briefs."

"Briefs," Will said matter-of-factly.

Tia and Jessica both blushed. "I can't believe you told me! Isn't that, like, betraying your fellow man or something?" Tia asked.

"He'll live," Will said with a shrug.

Tia laughed and leaned back as Jessica and Will discussed a pickup route. It felt good to focus on something other than Angel's weird behavior. Funny. Just a few days ago pulling off these kidnap plans would have been the bulk of her worries. Now it was a welcome diversion.

"Man, this is one bizarre tradition!" Will exclaimed.

"Yeah," Tia agreed. "We always thought El Carro was a party school, but we were never insane enough to come up with something like this."

Jessica sighed blithely. "I always knew SVH was cooler."

"You wish," Tia said, rolling her eyes.

"Nice comeback," Jessica quipped.

"Hey—"

"Wait a minute!" Will said. "Before you start cat-fighting—"

"Hey!" Tia and Jessica exclaimed in unison. Will laughed.

"I just have one more question," he said. "Where do we take everyone for breakfast?"

Jessica frowned. "Oh, yeah. I really don't know. We used to go to the Dairi Burger, but it was leveled in the quake."

"Hey. How about First and Ten?" Tia suggested.

A tense chill suddenly settled over the room, dousing the festive atmosphere. All the happy color drained from Jessica's face, leaving behind a decidedly unhappy pallor.

Uh-oh. Strike two, Tia scolded herself. She'd forgotten about the whole Jeremy episode.

"Uh . . . I don't know," Will mumbled. "Do they even *have* breakfast there?"

Tia nodded. "Yeah. On weekends they do." She paused and watched them staring down at the floor uncomfortably. Why'd she have to be such a ditz?

"Um . . . but if you guys would rather go somewhere else, we—"

"First and Ten will be fine. I'll call them and tell them to expect a crowd," Jessica said quietly. Then she quickly stood and checked her watch. "I really hate to rush you, Tia, but I think we should get going. We're pretty much done anyway."

"Oh. Sure. Okay," Tia agreed, glancing from Will to Jessica.

"I'll walk you guys out," Will said, standing up.

"No, that's okay." Jessica grabbed Tia's arm and steered her toward the door.

"Yeah. Thanks a lot, Will," Tia called out as Jessica dragged her into the hallway. "Bye!"

She practically had to run to follow Jessica through the house, out the front door, and over to the Jeep. Tia climbed into the passenger side and watched her friend warily. Jessica's hands shook as she fumbled with the keys, eventually dropping them onto the floorboard. Then she slumped toward the steering wheel and buried her face in her arms.

"Jess? Are you okay?" Tia whispered, reaching over to touch her shoulder lightly. "I'm sorry I made things weird in there. I'm a total airhead these days."

"No, it's not you," came Jessica's muffled voice. "It's me. I'm such a wimp! I just don't know what I'm doing anymore!"

"It's Will, isn't it?" Tia asked softly. "You really like him, huh?"

118

Jessica lifted her head and stared at her. "Yeah," she mumbled shakily.

Tia hesitated to ask the next obvious question, but curiosity got the better of her. "What about Jeremy?"

Jessica slouched back in her seat and stared at the windshield. "I don't know. I really care about him, but I think I might care about Will too." She touched her fingertips to her forehead and shut her eyes tightly. "The thing is, Jeremy's the one I need, but Will's the one I think I want. Or maybe Will's the one I need, and Jeremy's the one I think I want."

"Sounds like a tough call." Tia shook her head sympathetically.

"Should I do what I *think* is right? Or should I do what I *feel* is right?"

Tia sighed heavily. "I know exactly how you feel, Jess," she muttered gloomily. "But I can't help you. This is just one of those things you need to figure out on your own."

Elizabeth Wakefield
List of Jobs to Apply For

-Assistant at the library
   (No, wait. Scratch that. That was
where I first "met" Conner.)

-Clerk at MusicTown
   (Nope. Music reminds me of Conner.)

-Waitress
   (No. Food will only remind me of the
fact that I never went out on an
actual date with Conner.)

-Delivering newspapers
   (Uh-uh. Newspapers remind me of
notebook paper, which reminds me of
writing class, which reminds me of
Conner.)

–Cashier at the grocery store

(No way. Grocery stores will have magazines, which will remind me of Conner, and muscular stock boys, who will remind me of Conner, and headache medicine, which will remind me of Conner.)

I think I'll just be broke and bored and have a spotty resume and not be able to get into decent colleges and never amount to anything. So then no one will want to be around me and I'll be left dealing with everything alone.

Which, of course, will only remind me of Conner.

Maria Slater

Morning announcements

8:00 A.M.

May I have your attention, please?

Starting today, the student council will be selling spirit ribbons for the Palisades game. For only fifty cents you can show our colors and support our team. That's less than the cost of a soda in our vending machines. Remember that the proceeds from this fund-raiser will go toward the senior-prom fund—a very important cause.

Oh, and the administration wants me to remind you to wear your spirit ribbons appropriately. No pinning them to, uh, personal places on your outfit, no taping them to your forehead, and no spelling out rude words to flash at the opponents' cheering section. It is possible to support our team while demonstrating how responsible and mature we are as a school.

Let's all . . . I don't really have to read this part, do I? . . . Really? . . . Ookay . . . Let's all put the, _ahem,_ "Sweet" back into "Sweet Valley High." Thanks for listening. Go, Gladiators!

CHAPTER 8
Doing Time

"Have you ever wondered how many tax dollars are wasted so someone can stamp the word *inedible* on all the big cafeteria garbage cans?" Andy mused out loud. "I mean, do they really have a problem with lots of confused students digging through them for their lunch?"

"You think too much, Andy," Tia said wearily.

She couldn't believe it was only lunchtime. The morning had dragged on relentlessly, and the fact that she'd had her fifth sleepless night in a row didn't help matters much. All she wanted was some peace and quiet. Unfortunately, her choice of lunch mates made that impossible.

"*Andy* thinking too much?" Conner muttered. "I really doubt that's his problem."

Andy gave an exaggerated shrug. "Hey, I'm just trying to entertain here. You guys are about as much fun to eat with today as a couple of potted plants. What is *with* you?"

"Well, *some* of us are worried about Angel," Tia snapped.

123

"Oh, I see! Of course!" Andy's eyes widened in mock revelation. "Sitting around and moping is a *great* way to help him out. Gee. Why didn't I think of that?"

"Can you please just shut up, Andy?" Tia pleaded. "Just for one solid minute?"

"Of course I can. No problem. No big deal. But just let me say this first, and then I'll shut up. I expect Conner to be stoic man, but not you, Tia. You're the one who wanted to take action. You're the one who—"

"Hey!" Tia cut in. "It's not like I haven't tried! I've done everything I—" She sighed and stared down at her tray. "Right now all he needs is some space," she finished quietly, trying hard to regain her composure.

"Space?" Andy repeated. "You think he needs space right now? People living in downtown Tokyo need space. The LA freeways need space. But Angel? If you ask me—"

"I'm not!" Tia hissed through her teeth. In about five seconds she was going to launch across the table and stuff an entire apple in Andy's mouth to silence him. "One minute without talking, Andy. Please! Just sixty seconds!"

Andy pressed his lips together and lifted his watch.

Tia sighed. She knew she was acting like a pouty little kid. Even Conner was giving her wary looks.

But she couldn't help it. It had been days, and Angel still hadn't called to apologize. Obviously he was writing her off.

As much as she worried about him, she just couldn't bring herself to call him or see him. She wanted to help, but her presence only seemed to confuse him even more. Under other circumstances, his idea to stay out of school and be with her would have been music to her ears. But she knew it was just an easy excuse for him to avoid facing the mess he'd made. And Tia wanted to be part of the solution, not the problem.

"Conner," Tia said tentatively. "Have you talked to Angel lately?"

"Haven't you?" Conner asked, his brow creasing slightly.

"No," she said glumly, staring down at the red swirl pattern she was making with her fry in a blob of ketchup. She sensed Andy and Conner shooting each other looks.

"Tee?" Andy said. "I know I'm no honor student, but why aren't you spending every spare second with Angel? I mean, don't you think he needs . . . you know . . . you?"

"Look, it's not that easy," Tia said, tossing her french fry down on her plate. "I want to be there for him, but he refuses to do anything. And I can't just sit there and watch him do nothing."

"Why not?" Andy asked, looking directly into her eyes.

"Because! It's . . . it's just so *frustrating*. Nothing I say matters." She crossed her arms and leaned back in her chair. "I can't take seeing him like this."

Andy and Conner looked at each other again, then they both rolled their eyes and concentrated on their food. Tia felt a blush rising up her neck. Were they suddenly judging her?

"You guys," she added defensively. "There is a lot of stuff going on in *my* life too, you know. I'm totally swamped right now. I've got to get the cheerleading stuff ready for the game. I need to paint the banner, hang up the spirit posters, haul our equipment to the field. I'm under a lot of pressure."

She couldn't believe she'd just said that. Had she actually put poster painting in front of Angel?

"You just don't get it," she said wearily, slumping so low in her chair, she kicked Andy's foot with her sneaker.

"You're right. I don't understand," Andy said with a smirk. "Why do people go so crazy over sports anyway? I mean, they're just football players. I know they're called the Gladiators, but it's not like they're actually going off to battle or anything."

Tia exhaled slowly, glad Andy had changed subjects.

"You know, Andy. The reason you don't understand is that you have no school spirit," she said.

Andy and Conner groaned simultaneously.

"Oh, please," Andy said, rolling his eyes.

"Not this lecture again," Conner grumbled.

"I mean it!" Tia went on. "I love sports, and I love supporting the teams!"

"Let me ask you this," Andy said, leaning across the table toward her. "You still cheer the team on even when they're losing, right?"

"Of course!" Tia threw up her hands in frustration. "Even more so!"

Andy shrugged. "Then why don't you do that for Angel too?"

"Okay, Dave," Pat Sajak said to the short man in the blue suit. "Would you like to solve the puzzle?"

"Live long and prosper," Angel muttered.

"Live long and prosper!" the blue suit shouted, smiling gigantically.

The music swelled. People applauded. Blue suit's cash-award total flashed in giant white numbers.

"Man, this is easy," Angel said to the television. "Maybe I should go on the show. So what brings you on *Wheel of Fortune*, Angel?" he asked himself, doing a passing imitation of Pat Sajak's chronically cheerful voice. "I'm trying to win a life, Pat," he answered.

A commercial for lemon-fresh laundry detergent came on, and Angel realized with a groan that he practically had it memorized. He stretched and stood up from the couch, causing the hazy, prickly darkness of a major head rush to cloud his vision. Angel rubbed his eyes and glanced at the clock on the wall. Still three hours to go before his shift at the Riot started. He couldn't wait to get there.

I'm actually looking forward to slaving for Mr. Walker? he thought wryly. *How lame is that?*

At that moment his father lumbered through the front door. His hands and jumpsuit were stained with car grease, and his face looked completely drained of energy.

A paralyzing guilt flooded through Angel. He knew his dad was having to work twice as hard since he'd fired Angel. Maybe he'd changed his mind now that he realized how hard it was without Angel around.

Nervously smoothing down his green polo shirt, Angel took a step forward and cleared his throat. "Hey, Dad. How did it go today?"

His father unbuttoned the top button on his coveralls and wiped the sweat off his brow with the back of his forearm. Then he squinted at Angel, glanced over at the television, and flashed Angel a disdainful look. "It went fine," he said curtly.

"You, uh, seem tired," Angel pointed out.

No acknowledgment.

Angel awkwardly shoved his hands in his front pockets. "Uh . . . Dad? I was wondering. Since you're so swamped and all . . . and since I owe it to you anyway . . . what if I were to go back to work for you? I mean, you could give me a cut in pay—"

"No," Angel's dad said firmly.

Angel felt as if he'd been punched in the stomach, but he forced himself to continue. "Look, Dad. This is hard for you, working the whole shop by yourself. I can tell."

"That's *my* problem, not yours," his dad replied. "Not anymore."

The icy chill in his father's voice made Angel shudder. "God, Dad. Don't you respect me at all anymore?" he asked.

His father scowled. "Respect isn't automatic. It's earned. And if you want to earn back some respect, you can start by doing something for yourself instead of sitting around the house all day. Now, if you'll excuse me"—he turned into the hallway—"I'm going to get showered and cleaned up before dinner."

Angel watched his dad's hunched, and most likely aching, back disappear around the corner. He felt dirty and corrupt, as if he were the one in need of a good bath. Behind him he could hear Pat Sajak's gleeful announcement of a new word puzzle. An assortment of junk-food wrappers lay strewn across the coffee table. Angel caught a glimpse of his reflection in the foyer mirror. His eyes were red and baggy, and his shirt was untucked and covered with fragments of Doritos.

Dad's right, he thought dejectedly. *How can I expect people to treat me right when I've lost all pride in myself?*

Angel grabbed the remote and shut off the television, then smoothed the crumbs from his chest and tucked in his shirt. He looked better already. Now for something productive.

The morning newspaper poked out from underneath a pile of snack-food debris. Angel quickly dug it out and located the classified-ads section. It was time to get serious about working. After all, if he wasn't going to college, the job at the Riot wasn't enough to build a future on, especially a future for him *and* Tia—if she was still interested.

His index finger traced down the narrow columns of help-wanted ads. Fry cook. Usher at the movie theater. Pet groomer. Car-wash attendant. Nothing with any real money-making potential. Then a large, boxed ad toward the bottom of the page caught his eye.

Advanced Intersystems, Inc.

Do you want a job in the fast-moving and high-paying world of the computer industry? Our firm is currently hiring qualified individuals for a variety of positions. We offer competitive salaries, medical and dental, retirement benefits, and employee stock options. If this sounds like the environment for you, call 555-3891 today!

Angel felt his bad mood rising off him like vapor. *I could do this*, he thought brightly. His Stanford scholarship was based on his knowledge of computers. A job like this would be perfect.

He crossed the room and picked up the phone, his pulse racing. He would call and arrange an interview. Then if he got hired, maybe he could win back his dad's trust.

And hopefully Tia's.

Ken took off his T-shirt and used it to towel the sweat off his head and neck. Then he picked up his telephone and dialed Maria's number.

"Hello?"

"Maria! Hey! It's Ken!"

"Ken! How are you?" Maria asked in her typically cheerful tone. "How did football practice go today?"

"Unbelievable! I've got a black eye, some bruised ribs, and I might never walk again. It was great!"

Maria laughed. "Boys. You just love your contact sports."

"Sad but true," Ken said. He tossed his dirty T-shirt across the room and gingerly sat down on his bed, listening to the sound of his bones cracking back into place. Somehow the sound made him even happier.

"How was the team?" Maria asked.

"Merciless," Ken said. They'd never let up once during the three-hour-long practice. But Ken was

131

getting better at avoiding the fierce tackles, and his buddies were really looking out for him. He might be exhausted and sore, but he also felt more alive and capable than he had in a long, long time.

"Anyway," Ken said, carefully rotating his shoulder, "thanks for making me go back there. I might end up in the hospital, but I think it's good that I didn't back down."

"No problem," Maria replied. He could tell from her voice that she was grinning. "Just give 'em hell."

"Actually, they're giving *me* hell," Ken said. He lay back on his bed and smiled up at the ceiling. "But it's exactly what I needed."

Andy Marsden

"Channeling the Great Spirit"
(an essay for the Oracle)

It's that time again. Football is in high season. There's the upcoming game with our Palisades archrivals, homecoming a few weeks after that, and even talk of a district championship. You can almost smell the blood thirst in the air.

And football isn't the only manifestation of this us-against-them mentality sweeping through Sweet Valley High. People everywhere are kicking, spiking, dribbling, running, tumbling, serving, butterflying, birdieing, and home running all in the name of "school spirit." There seems to be a pervading belief that each of us shouldn't just root for the school, but also commit our physical bodies to it.

But let's face it—many students just aren't athletically inclined. In fact, some of us wish we could count channel surfing as a PE credit. So is it fair to say that the sports challenged among us have less school spirit than the jocks? I say no!

Okay. So I'm not out there on the front lines at our football games, but at least I go to them. And I'm new to SOH this year, so I don't know the words to the school song yet. But as soon as I do, I'm sure it will move me to tears as I belt it out with pride (or at least move those unfortunate enough to sit close by to tears). Despite all these things, I do feel tied to these great academic halls, and I resent people implying otherwise.

You say, "So what if you're not a jock? Get involved! Be a joiner! Prove your devotion through one of our many nonsporty clubs and organizations!" To that I say: Been there, tried that. I heard that the French club threw great parties, and I thought about joining, but then I heard you actually had to <u>take</u> French. Blatant discrimination. Then I found out the student council got to go on a field trip to Disney World, but after one endless yak session over selling candy versus selling gift wrap as a fund-raiser, I thought my brain was going to melt out my ear. Besides, it cut into my Internet time.

"Slacker!" you say. "Miscreant! How dare you shun the opportunities SOH has to offer a thankless thug like you?" But believe it or not, I do feel a sense of loyalty toward this place. And I don't need to pigeonhole myself with any extracurricular activities in order to prove it.

You see, school spirit is just that: It's spiritual, in that it is very private and sometimes unseen. So remember, even though some of us may not attend lots of meetings or body-slam rival competitors in the quest of a holy SOH victory, that doesn't mean our hearts are not full of reverence. We are still human beings— more so, even, since we are happy to simply "be" here. The rest of you are human "doings." You are so busy with your sports and activities that you don't take time to enjoy the Zen of the SOH student experience.

We, the lazy and uncoordinated,

demand respect. We demand it nicely, and we won't muster up the energy to march down Main Street, but we demand it nonetheless. Please don't waste your valuable club and practice time worrying about our support for the school. We're here, aren't we?

Oh, and by the way . . .

Go, team!

May the Best Man Win

Angel shifted restlessly in the giant leather armchair, watching as Mr. Banks scrutinized his resume as if it were some rare and valuable artifact.

"Very nice. Good. Good." Mr. Banks nodded down at the paper.

The interview had gone incredibly well. Every answer Angel gave seemed to please the guy, and he'd laughed heartily when Angel described his "reliable transportation" as a car that was "only one notch slower than the Concorde, but just as noisy."

Of course, Angel also made sure to leave out any mention of his gambling, his dad's firing him from the shop, and his decision to turn down Stanford. He was fairly certain Mr. Banks wouldn't understand or sympathize with the complexity of the situation. As far as he was concerned, Angel was a bright kid with an aptitude for computers; nothing else. And Angel wanted to keep it that way.

"Well, I have to say I'm impressed." Mr. Banks set down Angel's resume and leaned forward in his chair, clasping his hands in prayerlike formation.

"You seem very responsible and mature, and your experience shows you to be hardworking as well."

Angel smiled awkwardly, feeling a little like a fraud. Everything the man said *used* to be true. But maybe it still was. Maybe all he needed was a chance to prove himself.

"As far as I'm concerned," Mr. Banks continued, "you can come on board anytime you're ready." He pushed back his chair and stood up, holding out his hand toward Angel.

"Really?" An intense relief flooded through Angel. This was it! He'd actually done it! "Thanks!" he gushed, grabbing Mr. Banks's hand and vigorously pumping it up and down.

Mr. Banks laughed. "I like the enthusiasm. Now, how about I give you a brief tour of the facilities and maybe familiarize you with the workload?"

"Sounds great," Angel replied.

He followed Mr. Banks out of the office and into the main workroom, feeling Christmas-morning giddy. He was about to find out about his future.

Rows of tiny cubicles, each with its own desk and computer terminal, crisscrossed the room. At each station a man or woman sat hunched behind a monitor, busily clacking away at a keyboard or talking on the phone in dense, hard-to-follow computer jargon. A steady hum of machines and human chatter filled the air. To Angel, it sounded like beautiful music.

Glancing about, he wondered which cubicle

would be his. He imagined himself sitting in one of the three-sided boxes with his suit jacket on the back of his chair and a photo of Tia on the desk in front of him. At last he could quit his job at the Riot and free up his evenings. Then, as soon as the cash started rolling in, he could start paying back his father for the investment he made into his college fund and maybe save a little to take Tia out for an occasional dinner or movie. He'd have a life again. A purpose.

"This is it," Mr. Banks announced, gesturing around the workroom. "Every Thursday is trash day, so you would have to remember to empty all the garbage into the Dumpster on Wednesday afternoons. Over here we have our stockroom. You would need to resupply materials as needed."

A cold feeling of dread started in the pit of Angel's stomach and worked its way through his veins. What was this guy talking about?

Mr. Banks pointed to a couple of tall, cylindrical bins. "On Fridays the recycling truck comes by. That means you'll need to—"

"Um, excuse me, Mr. Banks," Angel interrupted. "I think there's been some sort of mistake. You see, I . . . I was applying for one of the system-support jobs."

"Oh?" The friendly expression fell from Mr. Banks's face, replaced by a look of pity. "Oh. I see. I'm sorry. But I'm afraid I can't hire you for that. As a matter of policy, we require degrees from college or technical schools for all of our system-support specialists."

"Oh." Angel suddenly felt hollow. "I, uh . . . I understand," he said softly.

"Of course, that requirement can be waived with the right experience," Mr. Banks added. "If you work hard and attend a few training sessions outside of the job, you might be able to move up in a few years."

A few years? Angel felt his former hopelessness creep back into place. Why had he let himself get all excited? What made him think he could get a break?

"Why don't you sleep on it?" Mr. Banks said with a chummy pat on the back. "We've got a lot to offer here at AI. Take the weekend to think it over and call me on Monday. All right?"

Angel managed a weak smile. "Okay," he mumbled. "I'll think about it."

Then he turned and headed quickly out of the room before anyone could notice the moisture in his eyes.

Ken heard the snap, sidestepped Kavanaugh, and raced downfield. As soon as he was in position, he turned to see Will pull back his arm. A second later the ball was spiraling through the air in his direction. He could tell there was too much power behind it, but he still had to try for the catch. He stretched out his arms, hoping to get his fingers on the ball, but it was no use. The pigskin was still two yards out of reach.

And Ken was fair game for a tackle.

Ummpfh! Kavanaugh's rock-solid shoulder collided with Ken's chest, and the grass tilted up to meet his face.

"Whatsamatter, Matthews?" Kavanaugh warbled as he pushed himself upright. "Blow the play again?" Then he let out a mooselike laugh and loped back to his teammates.

Chris Policastro, the team's tailback, walked over and held a hand out to Ken. Ken grasped it and pulled himself up.

"Man, this sucks," Ken muttered, picking the grass and mud out of his face mask. "Those guys are determined to keep me out of the action. Kavanaugh's always tackling me right after the snap, and Coach never calls him on it. And when I do get downfield, Will purposely overthrows so I'll get creamed."

"I know. It's low," Chris said, nodding. "But it's only because you've been making them look bad these past couple of practices."

"Well, they sure got my number today," Ken mumbled. He leaned down and covertly rubbed his left knee. If nothing else, he was determined not to reveal his aches and pains to the El Carro guys. Let them wonder.

"You aren't thinking about giving up, are you?" Chris asked.

"No way, man." Ken shook his head. "But how can I prove myself to Coach if they're always ganging up on me?"

"You know, Matthews, I have an idea." Chris smiled slyly. "The next play is supposed to be the 36 Toss Sweep. You just get downfield, and I'll do the rest."

Will hollered for them to join the huddle, and Ken and Chris jogged over and nosed their way into the group.

Sure enough, Will called the 36 Sweep. Ken remembered it well—the quarterback pitched the ball laterally to the tailback, who then followed the fullback into the hole. It usually guaranteed a good five or six yards.

The huddle broke, and Ken took his position directly opposite Kavanaugh's leering frame. Hearing the snap, he immediately veered left and charged thirty yards downfield, leaving Kavanaugh with nothing but air. He turned and saw Will toss the ball to Chris. But instead of following the fullback into the hole, Chris paused briefly, spotted Ken, and launched him a long, wobbly pass.

Since the defense had counted on a running play, Ken was wide open. And Kavanaugh was still a good ten yards back. Holding out his hands, Ken easily snatched the ball out of the air, turned, and ran the next couple of yards into the end zone.

"Yes!" He turned around and held up the football for all to see.

A long whistle suddenly pierced the air, and Coach Riley stalked onto the field. "Policastro and Matthews, over here! *Now!* The rest of you hit the showers!"

As Ken and Chris slowly ambled toward the coach, the rest of the team took their time heading into the locker room. Will gave Ken a dirty look, and Amos Kavanaugh smirked and made a throat-slashing motion with his finger. But Ken didn't mind. Making the play was worth any chew-out session Coach had to offer. *Way* worth it.

Coach focused on Chris first. "What the hell do you think you're doing, Policastro?" he hollered, thick veins emerging from the side of his neck. "When I ask for the 36 Toss, I want the 36 Toss, not the 36 Halfback Pass! Understand?"

"Yes, Coach," Chris muttered to his cleats.

"You are not the quarterback on this team, and you are not the coach! You will run every play that is called just like it's supposed to be run. And if I see any more crazy stunts like that, your butt is mine. Got that?"

"Yes, Coach."

"Now get out of my face and hit the showers!"

As Chris trudged off toward the locker room, Ken flashed him an apologetic look. But Chris just smiled and shook his head. Then he pointed at Coach's back and mouthed, "Good luck."

"Matthews!" Coach Riley turned his steely gaze on Ken.

Ken instinctively squared his shoulders. Deep down, he knew he had little to fear. After all, Coach couldn't exactly throw him off the team when he wasn't even on it. But it was hard to shake off two years of dreading such a face-off.

"Yes, Coach?" he replied. He braced himself for the imminent "you're too much of a distraction" or "you don't belong here anymore" speech, trying to think of a possible defense. He hadn't come this far just to get tossed out again.

Coach regarded Ken with a fierce squint, as if he could penetrate Ken's outer layers by sheer visual concentration. Then he exhaled loudly.

"Let's get some things straight," he said. "If you show up for every single practice and continue to work out twice as hard as the rest of the guys, then you *might* be allowed to ride the bench as a second stringer for the rest of the season."

"Seriously?" Ken said. Then he caught himself and tried to stifle his smile. But it wasn't easy.

Coach held up a hand. "Now, don't get ahead of yourself here. You can show up for the game tomorrow night and watch the action from the sidelines. But you better not suit up. Not yet."

"Right, Coach," Ken said, nodding. "Don't worry about me. I just want to do my part, whatever you say that is."

"Good," Coach said, grabbing his clipboard. "Now hit the showers!"

Ken unhooked his helmet and trotted off toward the locker room. His body felt inexplicably light, and he could barely feel his legs beneath him. He wasn't sure if the numbness was caused by joy or the countless poundings by El Carro linemen. But it didn't matter. He'd done it. He'd finally fought his way back onto the team.

Let's see. . . . Spider is to web like bird is to nest. Okay, that one was easy.

Contentment is to purr like . . . terror is to scream? Sleep is to snore? Excoriation is to yelp?

What the heck is excoriation anyway?

Jessica doodled absently in the margins of her notebook. Good ol' Mrs. O'Reilly and her analogies. As far as Jessica could tell, the only things in life that required these problems were SAT tests and ancient English teachers. So why bother? It seemed like a major waste of TV-watching time. Besides, they were too hard.

"Just look at the given set and find the relationship!" Mrs. O'Reilly had said over and over. "Then you'll understand which answer choice is best."

Yeah, right, Jessica thought ruefully. *Like it's that easy.* Of course, Mrs. O'Reilly probably did analogies for fun.

She pushed her notebook aside and yawned.

"Studying is to Jessica what sleeping pills are to the rest of the human race." Yep. It was definitely time to stop.

Okay. So she had no date and nothing to do but get caught up on her studies. So what? At least she wasn't sitting around moping about the Jeremy versus Will deal. In fact, she'd managed not to think about it all evening. That is, unless thinking about *not* thinking about it counted as thinking about it.

Jessica groaned, slumping over her desk with her head resting on her arms. She just couldn't pretend everything was okay anymore. She'd always marveled at the way Elizabeth managed to contain her emotions and wondered if it could work for herself. But it was way too hard. Besides, what was so wrong about feeling sorry for yourself? What was the point of having these feelings if you couldn't cry and scream and hug a pillow? Acting out seemed every bit as therapeutic—and twice as satisfying—as turning to stone. And Jessica was good at acting out.

If only Jeremy realized that. He'd called things off between them in order to give her time to think. But Jessica preferred *doing* over thinking. The problem was, so far she had no idea what to do.

"At least I didn't kiss Will," Jessica muttered to herself, feeling her heart pang with regret as she remembered the warmth of his arms, his breath, his voice.

Whimper.

Somehow she had also managed to avoid Will the rest of the week. She'd slouched behind her huge textbook all through history class and taken alternate routes through the hallways if she knew there was a chance of meeting him. Plus whenever she found herself daydreaming about their slow dance, she'd automatically switch mental channels to scenes of Jeremy.

Jeremy was still ahead in the race—if there was a race. Now if she could just hold out a little longer, Jeremy would eventually see how serious she was about him and they could get back together. Either that or Will would eventually slip up and do something terrible or get frustrated with her and go after some other girl. Then Jessica would know for sure she was making the right decision.

"I hope it happens soon," she whispered against the cold surface of the desk. "I can't handle doing nothing much longer."

The phone rang right next to her ear, and Jessica sat up straight. She quickly snatched the receiver before it could ring again.

"H-Hello?" she said, trying to slow down her heartbeat.

"Jessica? It's me, Will."

"Will?" Her heart immediately started pounding again. She forced herself to sound cool and calm. *Don't start blabbing to him again. Don't give him a way in.* "Hey . . . what's up?"

"I just wanted to tell you that Todd Wilkins and Matt Wells said they'd drive on Sunday. And they've been effectively scared into secrecy."

"That's great," Jessica replied. "Annie told me and Tia she'd help out too."

"All right. So we're good to go."

Jessica nodded. "Yep. We're all set."

A short pause followed. Good. The conversation was obviously at an end. Jessica applauded herself for keeping such a businesslike tone. Once again it looked like she'd make it into the clear.

"So . . . ," he murmured. "Been listening to any Sinatra?"

A tingly warmth fluttered through her. "No," she answered softly. "Not lately."

Another pause ensued. But this one was full of unspoken meaning. Jessica could feel herself crumbling.

No! she thought suddenly. *Don't go there! Get out while you can!*

"Uh . . . anyway, Will, I really have to go now. But thanks for calling. See you Sunday." Then before he could respond, Jessica punched the power button, disconnecting the line. She sat clutching the receiver in both hands, staring at it in horror as if it were an unpinned grenade.

That was close. A few more seconds and she'd have been a goner, completely under his spell.

From here on out, she had to think about Jeremy.

She should remember how nice and easy things were with him. And how perfect they were for each other.

Just find the relationship, she told herself, remembering Mrs. O'Reilly's instructions. *Jessica and Jeremy . . . Jeremy and Jessica . . .*

Jessica is to Jeremy what . . . Will is to Jessica? Jeremy is to Jessica what Jessica is to Will? Jessica is to . . . is to . . .

Ugh!

Sometimes there just was no answer.

melissa Fox

You want to know an undeniable truth about life? Gossip is good.

Don't get me wrong—I don't make a hobby out of spreading vicious rumors. That's more Gina and Cherie's territory. But I will place certain facts with certain people if I feel it will serve me well. It's like gardening. Just plant a seed, give it a couple of days, and soon it will sprout into a little drama all its own.

Recently I heard something interesting from a couple of reliable sources. It seems Jeremy Aames has broken up with Jessica Wakefield. Good. That ought to keep her occupied for a while.

You might think I should freak out about their breakup now that Jessica's free for Will. But I know better. You see, Jessica will want the guy she can't have—just like she wanted Will when he was mine. Now that Will is available and Jeremy wants nothing to do with her, she will naturally see Jeremy as the greater catch.

Moron.

And all this will not be lost on Will. Finally he'll be able to see what a shallow slut Jessica really is. Because even though he likes competition on the football field, in real life he doesn't handle it well.

I, on the other hand, thrive on the stuff.

CHAPTER 10
TELLING

"You know who I think is sort of cute?" Maria said, reaching over to grab a fistful of popcorn from the bowl on the Fowlers' coffee table. "Vince Vaughn."

Tia lay stretched out on the Fowlers' giant, chintz-covered sofa, listening as her friends' animated chatter filled the room like background music. She was so tired, she could barely even partake in the conversation.

"Yeah, sure. If you like bad boys," Jessica replied. She sat down on the floor and crossed her legs into a lotus position. "Not me."

Maria pointed an accusing finger at Jessica. "Oh, come on," she said, her mouth full. "You like the dangerous types."

"Yeah, Jess," Tia said lightly. "I've heard about your past conquests. The list reads like a roll call for *America's Most Wanted*."

"Whatever." Jessica waved her hand, as if to erase the comment. "I *used* to like that type. Now I'm into more wholesome, sweet-faced guys."

"Like Jeremy Aames," Maria said. Tia shot a wary

look at Jessica, but her friend simply shrugged and lazily stretched her arms over her head. She was either a great actress, or she was actually getting over the Jeremy thing.

"I know," Maria continued. "But we're not talking date-worthy *boys*—we're talking dream-worthy *men*." She dropped a piece of popcorn down the front of her red cotton nightgown and shook it out the bottom.

Jessica laughed. "You're never even gonna land a date-worthy *boy* unless you work on your table manners," she said.

"Very funny," Maria said, taking a sip of her soda. "What about you, Liz?"

"You know she's faithful to Tom Cruise," Jessica said. "The girl owns every one of his movies."

Elizabeth shrugged absently. "Yeah. I guess. Tia hasn't answered yet."

"No comment," Tia said.

"What's your deal? You've barely said five words all night," Jessica said, leaning over to rummage through a pile of CDs. "Wasn't this ritual gathering of the females your idea?"

Tia yawned. "I guess cheering at the game took all the energy out of me." She stretched her arms out to her sides and closed her eyes. "I'm actually kinda sleepy."

"Speaking of sleepy," Jessica said, dropping a dance-mix CD and glancing at the mantel clock. "I'm going to bed."

"No way!" Maria protested as Jessica scrambled to her feet. "Already?"

"Yeah. Sorry," Jessica replied, pushing her blond hair back from her face. "I'm beat from the game too. And besides, I have to get up really early tomorrow and . . . work."

Jessica gave Tia an insider wink as she walked past the couch, and it took Tia a moment to process the meaning. Then she remembered the kidnap and stifled a groan.

She was going to have to get up in a few hours and cart a bunch of whining cheerleaders around in her parents' smelly minivan. Lovely. She should be sleeping again sometime next spring.

"All right, Jess. Be lame." Maria grinned devilishly. "Of course, this means everyone gets to gossip about you."

Jessica rolled her eyes, straightening the elastic waistline of her baggy, plaid pajama pants. "What else is new? Now, if you don't mind, I must bid you adieu." She waved her arm with a flourish and disappeared around the corner.

"You drama people," Elizabeth muttered, shaking her head. "Maybe I should turn in too. I'm beginning to feel like I don't belong."

"Whatever," Maria said, grabbing an Oreo and twisting it apart. She licked at the center and smiled. "The party isn't over just because Wakefield number two is a loser. As I recall, it was Tia's turn to give us a description of her ultimate."

"My ultimate?" Tia asked. She was busy watching the back of her eyelids.

"Your ultimate *guy!*" Maria said.

"She already *has* the ultimate guy," Elizabeth protested. "Angel's one of those rare, perfect specimens."

Maria flashed her a warning look.

Elizabeth's eyes widened guiltily. "Oh. I mean . . . uh . . . "

Maria dropped her Oreo on a napkin and pushed herself away from the table, leaning back against the couch. "What my inarticulate friend is *trying* to say is that Andy told us what Angel . . . did." Maria tilted back her head and looked up at Tia. "How is he?"

Tia felt her face grow hot. She really, really didn't want to talk about this right now. Just thinking about Angel made her stomach clench and her nerves twist up like fried wires. "Okay, I guess."

"Good," Elizabeth said. "But how are you?"

"Fine!" Tia replied a little too sharply. Elizabeth blinked and exchanged a concerned look with Maria. But Tia didn't care. Why couldn't they just drop it? There were thousands of other things they could talk about.

"Well, at least he has you." Maria smiled reassuringly. "I'm sure you guys can figure it out."

"Right," Tia mumbled absently. *At least he has me. . . .*

A jagged lump welled up in her throat, and suddenly all her pent-up guilt and frustration rose to the surface. She quickly threw her hands over her face, trying to stem the tide of emotions, but it was no use. Tia started to cry, right there in front of her friends. She hated that.

"Oh, God! I'm sorry!" Maria cried, pushing herself off the floor and plopping down next to Tia.

"We're gonna need tissues," Elizabeth said, jogging out of the room.

"We shouldn't have brought it up." Maria touched Tia's arm.

"I just don't know what to do," Tia said, wiping at her cheeks with the back of her hands and sniffling hard. She had to stop crying. Crying in public was not an option. "He's not acting like himself. He's not even trying to figure a way out. He says he doesn't want to go to school at all."

Maria wrapped her arm around Tia and lightly rubbed her back. Elizabeth returned with a box of tissues and handed them to Tia. Quickly Tia snatched three of the soft cloths out of the box and held them to her face. *Take deep breaths,* she told herself. *Just calm down.*

"I'm okay," she said finally. She flopped onto her side on the sofa, completely spent. A gloomy silence fell over them. Tia glanced at her friends' long faces and the half-eaten bowl of popcorn. Some girls' night. Nothing like a huge dose of reality to ruin a relaxing evening.

She was just about to excuse herself to go home, hoping Elizabeth and Maria could still salvage some fun, when Maria clapped.

"I got it!" she shouted.

"What?" Tia asked weakly. Her eyes were all puffy, heavy, and hot, and she could barely find her voice.

"When my sister went away to school, she got a position as an RA," Maria said giddily. "The program provides her with free room and board, and then she gets a refund check from her scholarship fund to live off of. Why couldn't Angel do the same thing?"

Tia sat up quickly and waited for the inevitable head rush to pass. "Seriously?" she asked. "Do you really think that's possible?"

"Why not?" Elizabeth said with a shrug. "Angel's a good student, and he's really responsible. You should find out if his school has a program like that."

Tia felt her nerves start to untangle as a new feeling of hope slowly seeped through her. This could work! This could really be a way out!

She jumped to her feet and grabbed her bag. "I have to go talk to him," she said, looking at her friends. "Do you mind?"

"Of course not," Maria said, blushing happily. "I'm just glad I thought of it."

"Me too," Tia said, hugging her friend tightly. "You have no idea how glad."

Conner heard a series of thunks on the staircase. He knew what it was without looking. Without even opening up his bedroom door, he could identify the sounds.

His mother had finally been dropped off.

He had waited around for her all evening. Instead of hanging out having fun like any normal person on a Saturday night, Conner remained at home, waiting to hear if his mom had had any success with her charity pals. Her fancy dinner meeting had started at six. Conner glanced at the digital clock on his desk. It was now eleven.

The thunks sounded again. Heavy and irregular.

"Not tonight," he muttered, squeezing his eyes shut.

He set down his guitar and walked out of his room, peering down the hallway toward the stairs.

Sure enough, his mother was teetering awkwardly up the steps, bumping from one side of the railing to the other like a giant pinball. She was completely trashed.

So much for Mrs. Sitcom. His real mother was back in full force. And Conner couldn't make her disappear with the point of a remote control.

"Nice dinner?" he asked snidely.

Mrs. Sandborn looked up at him, startled, and nearly lost her balance. "Conner! You still awake, baby?"

"More than you," he muttered, clenching his fists at his sides. He could smell her from three yards away.

"Don't start." She reached the second-story landing and faced him with a wobbly frown, narrowing her bloodshot eyes.

"How'd the meeting go?" he asked. If there was a shred of good news to be had, he was going to squeeze it out of her. Then he'd go into his room and shut her out, just like he'd been doing every night for the past three years.

Mrs. Sandborn rolled her eyes and almost fell over from the effort. Part of Conner wanted to reach and grab her to keep her from hurting herself. Another, more pained part wished she would hit her face on the way down.

"It was so boring! God! It went on and on and on and on and on and on and on. . . ."

I know the feeling, Conner thought. But he wasn't ready to give up yet. She was probably sober for at least part of the meeting, which meant she still could have made an appeal to help Angel.

"Mom," he said, trying to make eye contact. Impossible. "Did you get the scholarship for Angel?"

She cocked her head and looked confused. "Angel?" she echoed. Then recognition slid across her features and disappeared. She brought a hand to her forehead. "Oh, that! Yeah. No. I forgot."

Conner felt his heart grow cold. Colder, if possible, than it had ever felt before.

"Why do I bother?" he snapped.

Mrs. Sandborn gripped her head at the temples

and closed her eyes. "Stop yelling," she whined.

"Don't tell me what to do!" Conner shouted. "You're such a screwup, Mom! You have no right to *ever* tell me what to do!"

She wavered slightly, teetering from foot to foot. "I'm your mother—"

"You're nothing!" Conner yelled, causing her to close her eyes in pain. "Nothing!"

He was seething now. Getting right in his mother's pathetically slack face. A tiny voice inside his head told him to drop it. Reel it in like he always did. She wouldn't remember this in the morning anyway. But a new jet of anger and disappointment sprouted up from some deeply buried reserves, igniting an uncontrollable rage. His muscles strained, and he felt like his eyes were going to pop out of his skull.

"It'll be ski season in hell before I come to you for anything again," he said.

"Conner?"

He felt his heart drop like a water balloon as he looked down the hall. Megan was standing in the doorway of her bedroom, her arms wrapped around her light blue nightshirt. Her white fingers gripping the cloth into balls at her sides.

Before Conner could say anything, his mother turned and started back down the stairs. She was moving so quickly, Conner was sure there was no way she'd make it to the bottom without tripping and tumbling down. But she did.

"Mom?" Conner called out, fear seizing his chest.

The only answer was the slam of the front door and the sound of screeching tires.

Tia pulled her mother's minivan into her driveway and hopped out, almost forgetting to shut the driver-side door. Then she raced into the house and hurried, as quietly as possible, to her bedroom.

She was all purpose. Her body was as taut as a cocked bowstring waiting for an arrow to be released. Just waiting for the words.

Angel's college papers lay on her desk, half illuminated by the moonlight streaming through her window. It looked sacred, somehow, almost prophetic. An ancient text that held the secrets to Angel's future.

You're such a dork, Tia chided herself. *Just get to work.*

Tia switched on the overhead light and began flipping through the pages, closely scrutinizing each sheet. Finally she struck gold. She held up a letter from the university's work-study office.

"Let's see," she mumbled, skimming over a bold-faced paragraph near the bottom of the paper. "Resident-administrator positions still available for second semester. . . . Final candidates will be selected through an interview process, followed by one-week training session. . . . Interested applicants should fill out attached forms by the date listed."

Tia checked the deadline for the application. It was in six days.

There's still time!

She had to let Angel know as soon as possible. Tia checked the clock. He should be home from the Riot by now. She grabbed her phone and started dialing his number, but just as she was about to hit the final key, her stomach took an unexpected nervous turn and she paused.

Did she really want this? After all, this could be her big chance. If she didn't tell Angel about the RA positions, he would have to stay in El Carro. That meant she could see him every day. They would never have to be apart again. All the fears she'd had about him going away to college would be moot.

"No," she said aloud, sitting up straight. She couldn't let Angel's future get away from him if she could somehow prevent it. She'd never forgive herself.

Tia quickly jotted down a note for her parents in case they woke up. Then she snatched her mother's keys again and headed out the front door.

Forget the phone. She wanted to see Angel's face when she told him. Besides, she *needed* to be there— just like she should have been all along.

Senior Poll Category #3:
Most Athletic

Jessica Wakefield — ~~Will Simmons~~, Todd
Wilkins and Jade Wu

Will Simmons — Will Simmons
and Cherie Reese

Elizabeth Wakefield—Todd Wilkins and
Tia Ramirez

Ken Matthews—Todd Wilkins and Maria
Slater

Maria Slater— Ken Matthews and
Jade Wu

TIA RAMIREZ—WILL SIMMONS
AND CHERIE REESE

melissa Fox—Will Simmons and
Cherie Reese

Conner McDermott—Evan Plummer and
Tia Ramirez

*Andy Marsden—Andy Marsden and Andy
Marsden*

The Way Things Should Be

Angel lay sprawled in the living-room recliner, hoping to find something meaningful in a late, late, late night B-grade horror movie. His shift at the Riot had been as dehumanizing as ever. Now all he wanted was to watch something mindless. Some bubble gum for the brain.

But just as the college football player was about to investigate the growling noise in the shed, there was a knock on Angel's front door.

"Let's just hope it's not a psycho killer," Angel muttered. He pushed himself up and walked out of the living room, listening as the football player got mauled behind him.

It was probably just Conner. Angel knew Mrs. Sandborn had gone to the big meeting that night. Maybe Conner had come by with some good news.

Angel took a deep breath and rested his hand on the doorknob. He wasn't exactly sure what defined good news these days. What would be so great about getting another scholarship and heading off to Stanford? Sure, he'd get an education and be able to build a career, but what did that matter after losing his parents' trust, his own self-respect, and the girl he loved? The damage had already been done. Nothing would change that.

Angel pulled open the door and was stunned to see Tia standing there, her eyes twinkling like gems under the porch light.

"Hey!" she said, smiling warmly.

"Tia," he whispered. He was so glad to see her, it hurt. "What . . . I mean, I didn't expect . . . I mean . . . what are you doing here so late?"

"I've got great news!" She pushed her way inside and thrust a few sheets of paper into his hands. "It's just what we've been looking for! A way for you to afford Stanford."

Angel's heart plummeted down to his feet. So *that's* why she'd come. She was still trying to get rid of him.

"Look, Tee. I know you think you're helping, but I don't want to hear it," he grumbled, walking back into the living room and tossing the papers on the coffee table.

Tia's smile fell from her face. "But . . . why?"

"Because it's obvious why you're really doing this," he said. "You just want me out of here."

"How can you say that?" Tia asked, dropping onto the arm of his father's favorite chair.

"How can I say it?" He threw up his hands in exasperation. "Come on, Tee. When I told you I wanted to stay behind and be with you, all you could do was complain. Then I don't hear from you in days. Looks to me like you're giving up on me."

Tia shook her head. "No! That's not true!"

Angel slumped against the back of the couch, ignoring her. "Maybe you never were all that serious about me," he mumbled, crossing his arms over his gray T-shirt. "Maybe you knew I was a loser all along."

"That's it." Tia's forehead creased up, and her eyes filled with tears. Angel noticed for the first time how unbelievably tired she looked. His heart responded with a pang. "I'm sorry I went AWOL this week, Angel," Tia continued. "But I wasn't pushing you away—I was just freaked out. I didn't know how to help you with this."

Her voice cracked, and she covered her eyes with a shaky hand. Angel wanted to scoop her tiny form up in his arms and comfort her. But he held back, afraid to risk his feelings any further.

Finally she looked up, blinking back the tears. "I've been dreading you leaving for Stanford ever since the day you got in," she said weakly. "But I kept it all inside and put on a happy face. Then after that night at the track, I *wanted* to believe you staying here was for the best, but I knew it wasn't." She snorted an awkward little laugh. "In a way, your losing the money made me realize more than ever that you have to go."

"What do you mean?" Angel said flatly, staring at the floor.

"I mean . . ." She walked over and stood in front of him, forcing him to look into her deep brown eyes. "I don't want to ditch your future, even if it means I have to let you go for a while. I want you to go *because* I love you, because it's the best thing for you. Besides, if you stayed here just for us, you'd only end up resenting me."

Angel gazed down at her shiny, tearstained face. His heart felt higher and lighter than it had in days. "How could I ever resent you?" he asked, swiping a renegade teardrop off her chin with his thumb.

She smiled crookedly, searching his eyes. "Well, I'd resent myself if I didn't do everything I could to get your butt to school."

Angel laughed and ran his hand over her long, wavy hair. "You're too good for me, you know?"

"Oh, I'm well aware," Tia said with a blithe shrug. She reached up and threw her arms around his neck, falling against him. Angel pulled her even closer, relieved to finally be back in her arms. He let out a long, low sigh. Tia pulled back and kissed him, soft and slow, on the lips.

"Now you *are* going to fill out those forms," she said firmly.

Angel's heart was lodged in his throat. He loved this girl more than life itself. He'd acted like a lunatic, and she was still here. Still looking at him the same way she had on their first date.

The least he could do for her was try.

"Right," he said. He slipped away from her and picked up the forms, glancing over them quickly. "You know you're saving my life here," he stated, dropping down on the couch and searching the clutter on the table for a pen.

"I know," Tia said, sitting next to him. "And I'm going to remind you of that every day for basically . . . well . . . forever."

"I can't believe you, Conner," Megan said, her voice filled with disdain. She was pacing the living room. Actually pacing. "How could you say that to Mom? What's wrong with you?"

Conner had to bite the inside of his cheek to keep from blowing up at his little sister. What was wrong with *him*? Was she kidding? But he knew she was just worried, and if her inner organs were in half the twisted wreckage his were, he didn't want to make it worse.

"Are you even going to say something?" Megan cried.

The phone rang, and they both jumped. Conner saw Megan start to move toward the telephone and he lunged for it, snatching it out of her grasp.

"Hello!" he answered, more exclamation than greeting.

"Yes, is this the Sandborn residence?" a cool, all-business voice asked.

Conner swallowed hard. "Yeah." His hands were shaking, and a weird, corrosive sensation burned in the pit of his stomach. His eyes met Megan's, and he watched hers widen with worry. *Not good,* his mind screamed. *Whatever this is, it can't be good.*

"I'm calling from St. Stephen's General Hospital," the emotionless voice continued. "We got this number off the identification of Mrs. Eleanore Sandborn, who was recently brought in."

Conner gripped the phone. He could barely stand. "How—? I mean, is she—? I mean, what happened?" he stammered.

"Sir, I'm afraid you better come down here as soon as possible," the voice replied with an impatient sigh. "Mrs. Sandborn has been injured in a car accident."

Jessica was nervously bouncing up and down on the balls of her feet, watching out the Fowlers' picture window as five cars pulled into the circular driveway. Tia's van, Todd's BMW, Annie's Mustang, Matt's pickup, and Will's Blazer. It was show time.

She raced to the hall mirror to adjust her clothes and reapply some lip gloss. That was the one good thing about being burdened with the kidnap. You didn't have Sweet Valley High's elite seeing you with a saggy morning face and Medusa hair.

Jessica opened up the door to let her partners in crime tiptoe inside.

"Hey!" Tia greeted her giddily.

"Did you leave early?" Jessica asked. "I went to look for you in Liz's room."

"I went over to Angel's," Tia said. "Everything's okay."

Jessica grinned and quickly hugged her friend. "Good. I knew you'd knock some sense into him."

Annie, Matt, and Todd came in next, followed by Will. A lawn of blond whiskers covered the lower half of his face, and his hair stuck out in messy tufts from underneath a baseball cap, but he still looked fantastic. Jessica felt her pulse accelerate as their eyes met. So much for remaining calm. Oh, well, at least she didn't have to be around him much since they both had to drive.

"Everyone have their list?" Jessica asked in a hushed voice.

They nodded.

"Let's get started," Matt said excitedly. "I can't wait to see Cherie's face."

"Annie and I have to get Lila first," Tia said, glancing at Jessica. "Which one is her bedroom?"

"Upstairs. Third door on the right," Jessica replied.

She watched the girls disappear up the staircase, leaving her alone with two guys she'd rather die than talk to and one she really, really *shouldn't* talk to.

"So . . . are you tired?" Will asked.

Jessica just shrugged, watching the staircase like a hawk.

"Lila's probably gonna freak, huh?" Will tried again. Jessica shrugged again. When was he going to get the message?

"Jess—"

Suddenly a loud noise emanated from the stairwell. Lila, with her hair matted and face covered in an avocado mask, was yelling at Tia and Annie as they marched her down the steps.

"Sorry, Lila," Tia sang out. "Can't wash up. That's the rules."

Jessica shot Todd a look, and they both stifled laughs. They knew Lila better than anyone in the room, and they both knew how painful this was for her. This was going to be more fun than Jessica had thought. *Maybe Melissa wears curlers and zit cream to bed,* Jessica hoped.

Everyone followed Tia and Annie outside, with Lila still muttering in protest. As they climbed into their cars and drove off toward the next victim's house, Jessica's heartbeat slowed to its regular rhythm. The hard part was over.

It took only a half hour before Jessica was completely caught up in the fun. By then the Jeep was half full of victims. Jade was there in her mother's red chenille robe. Jake Collins had on a T-shirt, striped pajama pants, and moccasin slippers. And after a brief debate they had let Chris Policastro wear sweats over the polka-dotted boxers he'd gone to bed in.

Jessica pulled up at a beige stucco house and parked behind Annie.

"Whose place is this?" Jade asked.

"Radinski's!" Chris cheered.

Everyone clambered out of the Jeep and joined the rest of the kidnappers on the porch. Will was at the front of the pack, and Jessica saw a wide grin light his face as Matt joined him. It suddenly occurred to her that she liked seeing Will happy.

Will placed a finger to his lips and turned the doorknob. As quietly as a dozen overtired people could manage—which wasn't all that quiet—they trudged into the dim living room and down a nearby hallway. Will paused at the door to Josh's bedroom.

"One . . . two . . . three," he mouthed. Then he flung open the door and yelled, "Pile on Josh!"

Jessica laughed out loud as everyone ran into the room and leaped on the bed in one gigantic mound. Jessica jumped into the sea of wriggling bodies, listening to Josh scream in protest.

"What the . . . ? Hey! Get off me!" he cried. "Get off me!"

"Mass tackle!" someone else yelled.

"Surprise!" Chris yelled. "You can stop dreaming, dude! It's us, not Julia Roberts."

As Josh hollered and struggled against the weight of the crowd, Jessica lost her balance. She tried to grab hold of an arm or a leg for support, but everyone was jerking around too quickly. The pile bucked upward, and Jessica found herself catapulted off the top. She landed with a muffled thud on the far side of the bed.

For a moment she lay there, giggling. Then another, much larger figure came flying off the bed, landing across her stomach.

"Ugh!" she groaned, feeling the breath squeeze out of her.

"Sorry!" her assailant exclaimed, scrambling about to face her. "Did I hurt—?"

It was Will. He was lying on top of her, supporting himself upright with his hands. His legs were tangled with hers, and his mouth, open in midsentence, was inches away from hers. Jessica couldn't have breathed if she tried.

She knew she should move. She knew she should push him away from her. But the warm feeling of his body pressed against hers, the mesmerizing blue-gray of his questioning eyes, prevented her from shifting a muscle. All other noises and movements seemed to melt away completely. There was only Will.

Suddenly the space between them diminished. Their lips touched, sampled, and joined together. Jessica closed her eyes as her pulse pounded in her ears. Why had she waited for this for so long?

Suddenly a sound broke through to her mind, ripping it open like flimsy gift wrap. "Let's go!" someone yelled.

Jessica's eyes snapped open and locked with Will's for a split second, then she pushed him away and they scrambled to their feet. Jessica hastily adjusted her clothes and mixed into the noisy activity. She was shaking from head to toe.

Her mind whirled as she raced outside with the others. She felt dizzy and disoriented, as if she'd just woken up after the deepest sleep. Climbing into the Jeep, she stole a quick glance over at Will. He was staring at her, but she couldn't tell what he was thinking. And she had *no* idea what she was thinking.

What was going on? What just happened? Did she really *kiss Will*?

"Oh, this is bad," she whispered under her breath. "Bad, bad, bad."

Unfortunately, she felt really, *really* good.

ANGEL DESMOND

7:32 A.M.

Unconditional love.

That's what this is.

That's what your parents are supposed to have for you, but mine don't. I messed up. I know that. But my parents stop talking to me? What kind of love is that?

Tia.

She's what it's all about.

She really did save my life.

CONNER MCDERMOTT

7:34 A.M.

I've handled a lot in the past. But I
don't know about this one. I just—
    I don't know.

JESSICA WAKEFIELD
7:36 A.M.

I keep trying to think about Jeremy.
Jeremy who never hurt me. Jeremy who never
lied. Jeremy who really cares about me. Jeremy
. . . Jeremy . . . Jeremy.

I keep trying.

But all I <u>can</u> think about is that kiss.

And how I <u>really</u> want to do it again.

ELIZABETH WAKEFIELD
8:08 A.M.

Another nothing day. I have nothing to do, nothing to look forward to, nothing to get excited about. Maybe I should just stay in bed.

After all, it's not like anyone's going to miss me. . . .

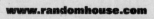